Chapter 1
East Berlin 1970

A win today would almost seal the title for us. I used to love big matches like this, with thousands of our Dynamo Berlin fans passionately bellowing out their support and getting behind the team. How things change. These days, football brings me nothing but an ice-cold emptiness. As I sit in the dressing room, I study the faces of my team-mates. How many of them feel the way I do? Who knows? In our team, we like to keep our cards close to our chests. It can be dangerous to show too much emotion. You never know who could be watching.

Our coach, Mr Muller, gives his usual team-talk. Muller's been at the club now for an eternity but is one of those people who never seem to get any older. I don't think any of the players would dare to ask him his age but I honestly think he could be anything between fifty and eighty-five. Sadly, and it hurts me to say this as there was a time when I'd have run through brick walls for him if he'd asked me to, but I'm not sure I can trust him anymore. Not after recent events. Muller gave me a lot of time and patience during my early career. He may have been a little frightening at times (there have been occasions when he's let rip at me with such ferocity, that I feared that he would physically attack me) but he's also shown a caring side and a loyalty to his players that you only really appreciate after working with him for a while. I guess you could say he's been a bit of a father figure to me. There was a time when I'd have entrusted this man with my life but I suspect he's let me down in the worst possible way.

I've no doubt that we will win today – no doubt whatsoever. In fact, I can't remember the last time we lost a match of any sort of significance. Dynamo have won the East German league and cup double now for four years in succession, a period of dominance that has never been seen before. Today we can all but secure the title and then in the next few days the club will have the biggest match in their history when they face St Etienne of France in the second leg of a European cup quarter final.

As we stand in the tunnel, with the whole stadium vibrating, I feel a hand on my shoulder.

"Everything alright Karl," Muller says, "his piercing dark eyes staring right into me."

"Fine Mr Muller," I lie, hoping that he has no way of reading my mind. "I feel good. I'll give you everything I've got."

And I will. Despite how I feel about this club, this country and everything they stand for, I just can't go out on the pitch and go through the motions. They'd see through me straight away and life would soon become very difficult. Not just for me either. There have been threats to my family about how uncomfortable life will become for them if I refuse to toe the line. That much is clear.

Just before kick-off, we gather in our traditional team huddle as our captain, Toni, barks out final instructions. I've known Toni since we were kids and he's the only person at the club that I feel that I can truly trust. We've had our disagreements over the years but he's been as good a friend to me as I could ever have wished for.

I can still remember the first time I lined up alongside him when we were just nine years old. Even then, I remember the passion he played with, chasing lost causes as if his life depended on it and showing incredible bravery when throwing himself into tackles against bigger boys. It wasn't long before Toni and I were absolutely inseparable, our minds totally consumed with playing football at the highest level. He became like a brother to me and we would spend hours kicking a ball around at the scruffy old concrete playground at the end of his street.

Normally I'd do anything for Toni but now his words go in one ear and out of the other. It isn't his fault – there's nothing anyone can say anymore that will make me fall in love with football again. No-one can undo what I've seen and heard over these last three years. So, when the whistle goes to begin the match, although I say and do all the right things, I couldn't care less whether we win this afternoon.

The first twenty minutes are utterly forgettable and drift by rapidly. Then, with almost the first sniff of possession I get, I receive the ball on the edge of the penalty area. With a quick drop of my shoulder, I buy myself a yard of space and strike the ball towards goal. It's not a bad hit but it doesn't get a chance to test out the goalkeeper as the opposition centre back throws his body in front of the shot and it catches him in the centre of his chest. Not one of our players appeal but there is a sudden, shrill blast of the referee's whistle and indicating a handball, he points to the penalty spot. A shocking decision like this used to surprise me but not anymore. It's happened so many times over the last few seasons that I almost expect it. Sometimes it can be a raised linesman's flag to disallow a perfectly good goal, or sometimes I've seen a clear foul by one of our players go mysteriously unpunished. Today, it's the generous award of a phantom penalty.

Nothing's ever said of course (no-one dares to) but we all know it happens. Dynamo Berlin have the officials in their pocket.

As the team's designated taker of spot kicks, I step forward in front of the whistling crowd. If only they knew that I'm as disgusted as they are. There's nothing I would like more than to blaze this penalty kick over the bar and high up into the stands but I know I can't. A deliberate mistake such would arouse suspicions and I've already been warned about my conduct.

I stand on the edge of the area as the rain, that has suddenly begun to stream down from the heavens, streaks down my face. I remember how my heart used to thump wildly when I used to take a penalty kick -the tension in my stomach, the explosion of sheer joy when the ball struck the back of the net. Today though, I don't feel a thing. I stagger my run and wait for their goalkeeper to commit himself, before reversing the ball into the opposite corner. In the stands, there is an eruption of noise and my team mates rush to embrace me. I accept their congratulations but can't help thinking of the freedom I used to feel when I walked out onto a football pitch. No matter how bad the week had been, Saturday's match was always an escape from the boredom of everyday life. Only now I'm not free any more. I'm as far from being free as you could possibly imagine.

I don't know how long the Stasi have had me under surveillance. It could be six months, a year, my whole life. What I do know is that I can't go anywhere or do anything without them watching me. Their tentacles seem to reach far and wide and it seems they'll resort to anything to keep me in check. And do you know the worst thing about it all? I'm almost certain that one of the team have been feeding them information all along. This breaks my heart. It truly does.

The rest of the first half isn't much of a spectacle really. If I'm honest, both sets of fans deserve to see a better standard of football from the two best teams in East Germany but perhaps understandably, our opponents have not taken kindly to the referee's penalty award and it turns out to be a somewhat spiteful affair. On at least two occasions, I am lucky to escape a serious injury after avoiding two footed lunges by their uncompromising centre back and the final whistle comes as a relief.

As I sit in the changing rooms, with Muller's words washing over me, I take a moment to think through my next move. It has to be the right one. One mistake could prove to be a disaster. I am suddenly filled with such a deep sorrow. I remember the first time Toni and I arrived at Dynamo's stadium. To become a football player was all we had ever dreamed of. How have things ended up like this? I think I'd have to go back to the very beginning and before the wall was built.

Chapter 2
Berlin
1950 - 1960

I was born in East Berlin in 1950, not that long after the conclusion of World War 2. I lived with my parents and my younger sister Heidi in a small two-roomed flat. It wasn't anything grand to say the least. All four of us slept in cramped conditions in one bedroom. It was extremely basic (we didn't even have hot water) but the war had left the country on its knees and we couldn't expect to be living a life of luxury. Although we didn't have much, I suppose we were quite a happy family and I enjoyed a settled childhood. I don't ever remember going hungry but then we were lucky as my father kept chickens and grew his own fruit and vegetables. That might not seem much but in those days all sorts of bartering took place within the neighbourhood and we were able to trade foods with other families and ensure we had enough to survive on.

I guess my family have good sporting genes. Before fighting in the war, my father had been a national standard swimmer while my mother used to compete as a sprint hurdler before she gave it up to settle down and start a family. From the moment I could walk, I would tear about our small home, bursting with energy and driving my beleaguered parents insane. As soon as I was old enough, my father took me to the local football club which happened to be run by a friend of his. Perhaps he hoped I could burn off my energy there and give him some sort of respite at home.

Right from the beginning, football brought me such a sense

of joy. Even at eight years old, I seemed to be able to glide past opponents at will and fire away powerful shots with my trusty left foot. Running had never been a problem for me either and I would fly up and down along the flanks from the first minute to the last. My father, being a man of relatively few words, didn't get carried away with the promise that I had displayed, although I knew that he was proud of me.

I must have been at the club a year before I met Toni for the first time. It was the first time I'd ever stepped out onto a football pitch and felt inferior to anyone. I have to be honest and admit that I didn't like Toni at first. My father had already mentioned that our club were taking on a new player so it wasn't a surprise to see a new face waiting outside the changing rooms on match-day. What I wasn't prepared for was how bossy this jumped up little upstart was.

"You," he said to me as we warmed up before the kick-off, "stay out on the left side and don't stray inside. I don't want you cutting off my space in the centre."

I was stunned at the nerve of this new boy barking out orders as if the team had been specifically built to fit around him. What a cheek! I remember thinking that he'd better be some player to back up this level of arrogance but it didn't take too long for me to realise that this boy not only talked a good game but played a good game too. His energy levels and commitment were like nothing I had ever witnessed before and he seemed to cover every blade of grass on the pitch. Wherever the ball seemed to be, you could guarantee that Toni would be there too. He seemed to have this inbuilt ability to anticipate where a ball would drop and then get there first, always thinking a step ahead of everybody else.

And then there was the talking. He never stopped. One minute he was organising the defence and explaining where they should position themselves at corners, and the next thing you knew he was standing in the centre of the pitch directing wingers to run into space or beckoning our striker to come and receive the ball to his feet. He even found time to talk to the referee, complimenting him on his decision making. Yes – Toni was exhausting to listen to, exhausting to play with and exhausting to play against, but there was no doubt that he was a very special player.

Although he irritated me immensely to begin with, it wasn't long before I started to warm to Toni. He may have been bossy but he was also an extremely unselfish player, always playing in a pass to someone who was in a better position rather than taking on a shot himself and taking just as much pleasure in creating a goal as he would when scoring himself.

If something was bothering you, he seemed to sense it and know exactly the right thing to say or do to help. It probably wasn't more than a month after we met when we became firm friends.

Toni and I may have attended different schools but they weren't very far apart and we would often meet up after lessons and join in with the very competitive five a side matches that took place on the concrete playground near Toni's home. In all the games of football that I've ever played in, I'd still rank these as amongst the toughest. Most of the boys who participated were considerably older than us and would waste no time in throwing their weight around, thundering into the sort of challenges that under different circumstances could be considered a physical assault and competing for the ball as if the world cup was at stake and not just playground bragging rights. It was a battle alright and if you weren't tough enough, then it wasn't worth showing your face in the first place. On several occasions, I would limp home with grazes covering my knees and elbows, having been sent tumbling to the concrete surface of the pitch. No bumps and bruises would stop me from returning the next day though and I honestly think that those playground matches shaped me as a football player. In time, the coaches at Dynamo, especially Mr Muller, may have polished the rough edges but those experiences playing against teenagers on that dusty, concrete pitch, toughened me up and played a vital part of my football education.

Chapter 3
1961

Two days after my eleventh birthday came the day that will never be forgotten. It would cost me my family.

One night in August 1961, we were awoken by the screaming of sirens and the frightening sound of steel clanking along the cobblestoned streets. I remember Heidi running to the window immediately, cautiously peeking through the curtains, her pale face painted with fear. I joined her in an instant and I'll never forget what I saw. At the front of a menacing procession, came the motorcycles, followed by jeeps and trucks full of grim-faced soldiers. Then, trundling onwards into the night, I caught sight of the monstrous, Russian built tanks. Where were they heading? What would they do?

That night, troops had positioned themselves along the sector border that separates East and West Germany. Upon reaching their destination, they began unloading rolls of barbed wire. Working through the night with picks and shovels, they followed their orders.

My mother and father had stayed up all night. In between restless bouts of sleep, I could hear them talking in the other room. Even to a young boy, the anxiety in their voices was unmistakeable. It frightened me. It must have been about six thirty when Heidi and I joined them and it wasn't long before we heard screams ring out from the streets. Louder and louder the cries came and I found myself following my parents outside, the fear and panic that flickered within my chest growing with every step.

All around me, people were crying and consoling each other.

One woman was wailing that her family was lost to her for good, while an elderly couple just stood there motionless, locked in a sorrowful embrace. As time passed, the truth emerged. A wall had been constructed. When I say wall, it was more of a barrier at first. The concrete blocks would arrive later and it didn't matter anyway. The East and West of the city were now divided with rumours spreading thick and fast. Apparently, thousands of guards armed with machine guns stood along the boundary that separated our torn city.

Of course, I was too young to fully understand the reasons at the time but in time I'd come to realise why the wall had been built. You see, after the war, Berlin had been split between the Soviets, who took control of the Eastern sector and the rest of the conquering allies (the USA, the UK and France), who controlled the West. Each would have their own ideals, but without going into too much detail, the West began to grow wealthier and wealthier whereas people in the East, where everything is shared out equally by the government, struggled to put food on the table. As a result of this, East Germany began to lose its most successful people to West Germany at an alarming rate. They figured that something had to be done.

While my mother and father made frantic attempts to contact my uncle, who lived in Western Berlin, I was left to my own devices. A little uncertain of what I should say or do, I met up with Toni at the playground. For once, we weren't interested in playing football. The events of the previous night were all anyone was talking about and we wanted to see them for ourselves. I suppose that along with a little fear, you could say there was a little excitement too. We didn't have to travel far and from a safe distance away, Toni and I watched as an angry crowd gathered on the Western side of the border. On the East, there was no-one but Toni and I.

"Schweine! Schweine! Pigs! Pigs!" they shouted, many of them shaking their fists.

Still young and innocent I suppose, I still couldn't quite make sense of what I was witnessing. I didn't feel safe either and began to have second thoughts about our little adventure.

"Come on," I said to Toni, "let's go home. I don't like this."

"Don't be a baby," he said quietly. "This is important Karl. This will be part of our history – right here – happening right now."

Standing impassively before the angry crowd, stood an endless row of soldiers, rifles or machine guns pressed against their chests. Just within our range of sight, a long way to our left, further troops busied themselves by carrying six-foot high rolls of barbed wire and long steel rods.

"Come on Toni," I pleaded again. "I want to go."

"Five more minutes Karl," he replied watching with fascination. "Just five more minutes."

We watched as the crowds grew larger and the atmosphere grew uglier. Finally, several blue trucks arrived, carrying riot police. Before the trucks had even stopped, they flung themselves into the crowd wielding long batons and striking anyone who happened to get in their way. It frightened the life out of me and all of a sudden Toni wasn't so brave either. To this day, I don't think I've seen him move faster as we covered the short distance to his house.

Chapter 4

As the days passed, I began to realise that the building of the wall would have a direct impact on my life. For example, My Uncle Mikael, who lived in Western Berlin, was now completely cut off from our family. We'd spent pretty much every other weekend at his house and Heidi and I loved spending time with our cousins who were similar to us in age. Maria was six years old and would spend hours running about with Heidi in the garden, while Marco, who was two years older than me, was a lively boy with a mischievous sense of fun. Although he wasn't so keen on football, we got on very well. My Uncle's house had a large garden with many thick trees towards the back, and I don't think there was a single one Marco and I hadn't attempted to climb. He was absolutely fearless, often shinning up branches until he was fifty feet or so above the ground. He'd then shout down to me as I clung on for dear life some twenty feet below.

But, with Western Berlin now completely cut off from our home in the East, there were no more visits to my uncle's house and no more pleasant afternoons playing in the garden with Maria and Marco. To begin with, I was a little disappointed that I wasn't able to enjoy visiting my cousins but perhaps naively, I thought it would just be a temporary thing. We couldn't even speak to each other on the phone as direct contact with relatives was forbidden. In fact, all calls were monitored and if you wanted to ring someone, you would have to contact the phone company for permission first. Even then, the authorities would be listening in. The only form of contact I would have with my uncle or my cousins for the next ten years would be a small parcel that they'd send our family every

Christmas. I remember really looking forward to this little package of goodies each year. Inside, there would be a few gifts that we considered greatly luxurious. This might include items such as chocolate cake, fancy sweets or even some sort of exotic fruit.

You may wonder why my parents hadn't decided to up and leave East Berlin while it was still relatively easy to defect to the West. Before the wall was constructed, it was easy enough for refugees to take a cab, bus or subway to an airport in one of the three West Berlin sectors, board an airliner and fly to West Germany. One in five East Germans had already done exactly that and I know my father had talked it over with my uncle often enough. He didn't agree with the politics promoted in East Germany and he was well aware that we would more than likely have a better standard of living in the West, but he had a steady job, a home and he simply wasn't in any rush to uproot his young family.

Perhaps he misjudged just how much East Germany was about to change but almost overnight it seemed different somehow. The army, the police – the whole climate suddenly seemed more aggressive. Previously, the government had been trying to persuade its citizens that they shouldn't leave the country and now they simply had no choice. I know my parents felt as if they were now trapped but there was no other choice but to conform. You had to be seen to be toeing the line or you would soon be singled out. If you wanted to keep hold of a decent job, a decent home or a decent education for your children then you voted for the Socialist party and ensured that it was clear that you had done so. The elections themselves were a pointless sham anyway – completely rigged and if you didn't vote, you'd soon get a knock on the door. Nothing seemed to be kept secret so my mother and father just played the game.

For once, Toni and I talked about something other than football.

"Do you believe the guards will actually shoot someone if they try and cross the border?" I remember asking him shortly after the wall had been built. "Surely they won't kill one of their own people."

"I wouldn't like to chance it," said Toni. "I guess we'll find out soon enough. You'd have to have some nerve to make a break for it though."

"I agree," I said. "Surely the West can't be so wonderful a place that you would risk your life to get there."

"I don't know Karl. I think there are plenty of folks who would do just that. My father even had to talk Lothar – Toni's eighteen-year old older brother – out of trying to leave the other night. I've never seen them argue so fiercely."

"But how would he get across the border?" I asked.

"Said he and two of his friends were going to try and swim across the river. My father nearly throttled him. Said that he'd be filled with bullets before he'd barely had time to get wet."

"Well I don't think I'll ever get to the stage when I'm prepared to swim through icy water while dodging machine gun fire," I said with a chuckle.

"No – I'm the same," said Toni.

As it turned out, to begin with, the border guards didn't make any great effort to stop any defectors during the first few days. Several men and women made death defying leaps from upper floor apartments and swam across rivers and lakes to freedom. Then, about two weeks after the wall had first appeared, with streams of refugees attempting to escape, the first killing was reported when a border guard shot a man who was swimming across a downtown canal.

I was shocked when I heard the news but sadly this then became the norm. Fatalities when attempting to cross the border became commonplace. There were rumours of daring rooftop escapes attempts that ended in tragedy, an acrobat who managed to reach the West by walking along a carefully constructed tightrope and almost unbelievably, a couple and their two children who sailed over the top in a hot-air balloon. You never knew which stories were true and which were pure fantasy. Sadly, one man was even murdered by guards after tunnelling back into East Germany in a desperate attempt to break his wife out of the country. Rumours began spreading that border guards were even awarded medals after successfully stopping escape attempts. In other words, they were honoured for killing innocent civilians.

Chapter 5

I could never say that things eventually returned to normal but after the initial shock that followed the building of the wall, I began to settle down and try to make the best of a difficult situation. I may not have been able to enjoy the fortnightly visits to see my cousins anymore but I still had Toni and I still had my football. With all of the recent developments, I hadn't even played a match for eight weeks, having to settle for kickabouts at the concrete playground. Even these games seemed to have lost a bit of their competitive edge and were far more subdued than before.

Finally, my father, who admittedly had other concerns, began to take me to training sessions again and it wasn't long before I had reclaimed my familiar position on the left wing. I have to admit that it took me a few games to shake off a little rustiness in my game but before long I was playing to the standard I knew I was capable of, whipping in dangerous crosses and running until my lungs felt that they were about to burst. After all the uncertainty of the last few months, it was good to be back on the pitch again.

It was around this time that Toni and I began to watch highlights of the Bundesliga on his small black and white television. Usually, there were just two state channels available in East Germany but Toni, with some help from his brother, had been a little creative and rigged up a makeshift aerial. Of course, you would be in quite a bit of trouble if you were unfortunate enough to be discovered by the authorities, but to be honest, everyone was doing it as it allowed you to receive West German TV. Although Toni and I didn't care for many of the programmes, it did allow us to watch the Saturday evening football highlights. Watching the Bundesliga, with some of the best players in the world on view, and large fanatical crowds, was a world away from the rather bland offerings of the East German top division.

I suppose the years after the wall was built should have been miserable for me and I certainly missed my cousins. However, although we didn't have much money and lived in a cramped household, I still had plenty to look forward too. With nothing inside the home to occupy me, I was forced to get outside in the fresh air and exercise every day. I had no problem with that as I believe that playing sports with your friends in the street, or the park, is what kids should be doing.

By the age of twelve, my life was completely consumed by football. During games, along with Toni, I was often the standout player and it wasn't long before we began being selected for the local area team. Even though this was a step up and I would be playing against better players, if anything, I seemed to raise my game even further. All of the most promising players in my age group had been handpicked for development and I was able to attend extra training sessions that were put on by the area team's coaches. These were far more intense than anything I'd been used to before but the hard work was worth it as my game seemed to go from strength to strength. I even began to put on a bit of muscle too, which helped me to hold off any defenders who could usually rely on knocking me off the ball.

With all the football I was now playing, it would have been easy to let the standard of my schoolwork drop but my parents kept me grounded. They made sure that before I took off for training, my homework assignments were up to date and I was ready for the following day's classes. At the time, I remember being extremely frustrated at their strict attitude towards my studies but I can certainly appreciate why they made sure I kept my head down and carried on working.

Some young football players can progress through a few different levels and be satisfied with their achievements. For me, this was never enough. I wanted to better myself in every match I played.

I even enjoyed the physical challenges too, taking pride in knocking off the seconds in the 400m timed runs our coaches were so fond of setting up. No sooner had I climbed one step, then I was reaching for the next one. Toni was the same and we used to drive each other on in training. Even though we were great friends, neither of us liked losing to the other. It was a friendly rivalry I suppose but then Toni was the only player I ever felt inferior to. Whereas I thought that, with a fair amount of good luck, I could possibly make it as a football player, I had no doubt whatsoever that Toni would. He was just a natural footballer and a natural leader too.

Finally, shortly before I turned fourteen, our big break arrived. After a particularly impressive showing against a representative eleven from Dresden, Toni and I were informed that we'd been selected for the school of excellence at the sporting club of Dynamo Berlin. It was the stuff that dreams are made of and I had the feeling that something special lay ahead.

Chapter 6

Signing for Club Dynamo was a massive deal for both me and my parents. The Friedrich-Ludwig-Jahn-Sportpark stadium in East Berlin (I know – it's quite a mouthful) was only about ten miles from our home but I would be required to leave home and live at the club for five days a week. I would only spend the weekends with my family. For a boy who was not yet fourteen years old, you can imagine that this was quite a frightening proposition and if it were not for the fact that Toni would be coming with me, I might not have found it within me to go at all. My parents were also extremely anxious about the situation but were also acutely aware that it was impossible to deny me such an opportunity.

So, in the end I went. If I was to have a serious crack at becoming a footballer then there was no other option really. Thankfully, it didn't take me too long to settle in. I was allocated a room with Toni and another boy named Ernst Fischer. During the week, the three of us lived in each other's pockets. Ernst was quite a shy character which was probably for the best as I'm not sure I could have coped with two room-mates talking my ears off every day.

Dynamo expected a lot from their young boarders and I had to grow up quickly in order to meet their expectations. Our room was required to be spotless or we would get a stern telling off and risk getting a mark against our names. We weren't allowed to leave items of clothing lying around and we had to ensure our beds were made and mop the bathroom floor every day. Neglecting any of these duties was unthinkable.

Club Dynamo didn't just limit itself to the development of football players either. Boarders who had earned a scholarship came from all sorts of sporting backgrounds such as athletics, swimming, cycling, gymnastics and volleyball. Anyone within a fifty square mile radius who showed any glimmer of sporting excellence, provided they lived East of the wall, was soon snapped up by the club. There were even Olympic champions living within the complex and it was difficult not to feel a little jealous of the extra privileges that they enjoyed. This mainly came in the form of food. For example, the club ran a highly organised system at meal-times, relying on colour codes to identify who should receive the finest dining experience. People who had red tokens (these were reserved for world or Olympic champions) would enjoy larger portions and a greater variety of fruit and vegetables whereas green token holders would have a less exciting plate put in front of them. Then, finally, there would be those of us who held blue tokens. We were the lowest on the food chain and would only receive basic and somewhat meagre rations. Our coaches would point this out to us regularly in an effort to motivate us to succeed. I suppose it worked too as it made us hungry (literally) to get to the very top.

Although we may have been selected for our talent on the football pitch, Dynamo considered our education of the utmost importance. Right from the beginning, it was made clear to us that if we didn't take our studies seriously, then we would be released from the club. Toni and I made sure we got our heads down and worked hard. To be honest, I quite enjoyed the lessons anyway and the club made sure we always got the best teachers to ensure we would learn quickly. In fact, at the end of each year, there would be a review of your progress, both academically and as a player. Dynamo were well known for being completely ruthless in discarding anyone who had not made enough progress and as the time began to approach, I remember that Ernst and I would worry about being asked to leave. I felt I had being doing well enough but I suppose it was only natural to consider the possibility of failing to achieve a favourable end of year report. Only Toni seemed oblivious to the possibility of being sent home, so sure was he of his importance to the team. I sometimes wished I had his self-belief. One night, with the lights out and Ernst's gentle snoring the only sound in the room, he whispered down at me from his top bunk.

"Karl, are you awake?"

"No," I replied, not really wanting any conversation.

"Karl," he persisted, "I know you. You're not yourself right now. Tell me what's on your mind."

"There's nothing wrong with me Toni," I said a little sharply. "I just need a good night's rest that's all and you're not helping matters. Can you just leave me in peace? Is that OK?

"OK."

We both lay there in the dark for a while but I was restless and couldn't get off to sleep. Toni wouldn't let things drop.

"You shouldn't worry so much Karl. There's no way the club will send you home. The coaches aren't fools."

I still needed convincing.

"I don't know Toni," I said, opening up at last." I'm not sure I've done enough. I think I could be on my way. I really do."

"Nonsense," he replied, dismissing my fears in an instant. "You're one of the best players we have. Anyone in their right mind can see that. Surely you don't think they'd want rid of you."

I'm not so sure Toni. I overheard the coaches talking about me during training this morning. Lacks power and lacks belief in himself they said. Knocked off the ball too easily as well."

"So what," Toni said casually. "You're getting stronger with every match and who needs power when you can dribble and finish like you can? You'll be here for the next fifteen years Karl. You mark my words."

"I don't know Toni..."

"Come on Karl. No more worrying," he said. "The coaches are right about one thing though. You do need more belief in yourself.

If you don't think you're good enough then no one else is going to either."

He was right of course. He usually was. I'd have to develop that side of my game. After all, the best players all have that air of confidence, as if they know they are on a different level. You can sense it as soon as they step out onto the pitch. Toni had it already. I promised myself that I'd have it too.

Chapter 7

Over the next two weeks, I made huge strides forward. I might have been a quiet character off the field but when I was on the pitch I was totally different. I even began to open my mouth a little more, directing the play and barking out orders in all directions. I could see the look of surprise on the face of the coaches and it felt good. I'll show them I thought to myself. And I did. Of the three matches I played during that period, we won all of them and I scored five goals and set up another two. I was flying but then disaster struck.

Just two minutes into our next game, Toni whipped a cross into the box. The opposing centre back headed the ball against the back of one of his own team-mates and it fell to the ground in front of the goalkeeper. With the previous night's heavy rainfall, the pitch was something of a bog and the ball, rather than bouncing back up, almost embedded itself in a thick layer of mud. In a heartbeat, I reacted, sliding a leg out in an attempt to divert the ball into the net. Unfortunately for me, the goalkeeper had other ideas. Desperately throwing his body forwards, he managed to reach the ball a split second before me, and in doing so managed to completely clean me out in the process.

Like most goalkeepers, he was a big lump and when you're hit by someone that large at that sort of speed you have to be pretty lucky to avoid an injury. On this occasion, I wasn't that lucky. The pain coming from my left ankle was excruciating and I was immediately aware that I was in trouble. Foolishly, I tried to get to my feet. Perhaps I'd be able to run it off, I thought to myself - maybe a bit of the physio's magic spray would work wonders and

I'd be able to get on with the game after a little breather. No chance – I couldn't put any weight whatsoever onto my left side and all I could do was collapse somewhat feebly onto the pitch. The next thing I knew I was stretched out on the small dressing room table while the physio tried to remove my boot without aggravating the injury any further.

"Don't be such a baby Karl," he said cheerfully, as he finally managed to squeeze it off and remove my sock.

When I glanced down at my ankle, I didn't feel a great deal better. It had swollen up like a balloon already and seemed to be throbbing before my eyes. At that particular moment, I didn't think I would ever walk again, let alone play football. It was a horrible, lonely feeling.

Lying in agony while the physio prodded and pulled at my ankle with all the delicacy of a mallet, I didn't feel very fortunate but as it turned out, things could have been a lot worse. Apparently, I had suffered no long- term damage, and although it would be extremely painful for a while, my twisted ligaments would recover in approximately six weeks. To be honest, I had mixed thoughts about this. On the one hand, I was grateful that I hadn't been injured as badly as first feared but on the flip side of the coin there was the awful knowledge that I'd miss the remainder of the season. It was the middle of March already and the season ended in May. Even if I recovered in five or six weeks, I wouldn't be ready to play competitively for at least a fortnight after that. So, there was not a lot I could do but wait and hope. Hope that I'd done enough to persuade the coaches to keep me on for another year at least. It was incredibly frustrating feeling so helpless and not even Toni's positive words could pick me up this time. I'd been playing the best football of my life and now, through no fault of my own, everything had blown up in my face. I was convinced I'd be sent home after my yearly review which was scheduled for the following week.

On the day of the review meetings, I felt physically sick. It was a pretty heartless process really and I don't think the club covered themselves in glory in the way they handled things. There were sixteen of us altogether. Sixteen anxious boys sat in a bleak, cold kit room waiting to be called in for a meeting that could see our dreams dashed forever. Even Toni looked on edge. It was a short walk to the coach's office and then, once the meeting had finished, each player would walk across the pitch (possibly for the final time) and out into the car-park. Through the window, there was a clear view of each boy making his way out of the training ground and you could predict how each conversation had panned out from the way someone either walked out with a spring in their step or trudged along miserably looking as if they carried a heavy weight on their shoulders.

I don't think each individual meeting lasted more than five minutes but I can tell you that it seemed like forever. Just waiting – not wanting to talk to anyone else – not even wanting to look at anyone else. Out of the first ten boys, I was pretty sure that eight had been sent home and only two had been kept on. This wasn't anything unusual as Dynamo normally only kept five or six players on at the end of the year. The rest were consigned to the footballing scrapheap so to speak. I think the coaches must have been running the order based on our dorm rooms as Toni, Ernst and I had still to go in. Three more boys went in to see the coaches and as far as I could tell, only one had received good news. Finally, I got the nod to go in. With a nervous smile at my two friends, I was on my way.

As soon as I walked through the door I received a shock. Sitting alongside our two youth team coaches was Mr Muller himself. The first team manager. The boss.

"Take a seat please Karl. This won't take long," he said.

I offered nothing in return. I only just managed to sit on the chair without falling off it. I tried telling myself to stay composed. Although I didn't really know Mr Muller very well, I was pretty sure he wouldn't be impressed by some teenage player shaking like a leaf in front of him. What was it Toni had said? If you don't believe in yourself, then no-one else will either.

Mr Muller had been Dynamo's manager for as long as anyone could recall. He was quite an intimidating sight too, with unusually large blue eyes surrounded by thick white eyebrows and bushy hair on the top of his head that seemed to spurt out in several different directions. It was common knowledge that he could be a hard man with a vicious tongue when riled and yet he was well liked too. Mr Muller was well known for giving his time freely to anyone who needed his help or even just wanted to talk. He was involved in running the football club from top to bottom and knew absolutely everything that went on within it. There was no doubt that he was a figure who commanded respect and now here he was, ready to decide my future.

"I'll be honest with you Karl," he said, getting straight to the point. "I'm just not sure what we should do with you. You have talent – of that I'm sure, but the reports I'm hearing tell me that you're not determined enough – not tough enough for this game of ours. What do you think?"

The words that began to flow out of my mouth were a surprise, as much to me as to Mr Muller.

"The coaches are right to an extent," I said, staring right into Mr Muller's huge blue eyes. "I wasn't tough enough to begin with. I haven't always believed in myself. That much was true to begin with but before I got injured, I was playing better football than anyone else. I'm ready to take the next step Mr Muller and if you decide that it's not going to be at Dynamo then I'll make it with another club. It'll be your loss though – I can promise you that."

With that, I sat back in my chair and waited. I think Mr Muller was a little taken aback. He wasn't used to any player speaking to him like that, let alone a nobody like me.

"Could you wait outside for a minute Karl?" he said at last. "I'd like to discuss things with my colleagues."

After what seemed like an eternity I was called back in.

"I'm going to give you a chance Karl," Mr Muller said. "I think you could do well if you get your head down and work hard. You aren't going to let me down are you?"

I shook my head. "I won't let you down Mr Muller. Thank you."

I walked across the pitch with a spring in my step and out into the car-park. Once I was past the gate, I sat down on the wall and puffed out my cheeks, a wave of relief washing over me. I think I must have just sat there in a daze for at least five minutes. Then it struck me. I'd completely forgotten about Toni and as I looked to my left, I could see him coming towards me. He was dragging his feet and moving as if the weight of the world was on his shoulders. For a moment, I was shocked. There was no way they could have released Toni. It made no sense. What was I going to say to him? I'd have to think of something quickly as he was no more than ten paces away from me. I watched as he lifted his head and saw the solemn look on his face spread gradually into a wide smile.

"I had you going there for a minute didn't I" he said. "They told me you were staying too."

I was laughing now too and pretended to throttle Toni's neck in mock anger. It may have been a stressful experience but things had turned out well in the end. I felt on top of the world but then I became aware of someone standing behind me. It was Ernst and the tears streaming down his face told me everything I needed to know. It was the last time I saw him.

Chapter 8

I'd promised Mr Muller that I wouldn't let him down and I
didn't. When the next season began, and with my injury having
completely healed, I hit the ground running. I had grown a fair bit
during the summer too (my trousers were now too short and my
shirts all too tight) and that little extra bit of strength really helped
my game. It wasn't long before the goals were flying in left, right
and centre and I became one of the hottest prospects at the club.
Mr Muller certainly thought so as he came to watch our youth
team matches frequently and even made a point of pulling me aside
for a chat after the game had finished.

"Still working hard I hope Karl," he'd say with a smile. "You're
going to score a lot of goals for me one day."

I hoped he was right and he didn't have to worry about my work
ethic. I felt I'd been given a second chance and was determined not
to waste it.

By the time we were seventeen, Toni and I were close to the
senior side. It was almost like a competition between us to see
who could get there first. I remember signing my first contract
for the club for a very small amount of money that was barely
enough to survive on but it didn't matter. I was happy doing what
I loved for a job. It may seem strange but Dynamo also required
us either to combine our football with an apprenticeship such as a
mechanic or an electrician, or alternatively we could continue with
our education. I opted to study physical education, thinking that
perhaps I could work as a school teacher one day when my football
career was done and dusted. Players in East Germany never retired
as rich men.

I was absolutely desperate to beat Toni to an appearance for the first team. He'd always made things look so easy and I didn't think it would do any harm for him to come second for once. Deep down, I didn't really think I could do it though so it was a pleasant surprise when Mr Muller told me that I'd be starting the next match against Lokomotive Leipzig. One of our regular strikers had torn his hamstring in the previous match. To be fair to him, Toni was very gracious in congratulating me on the call up. It was probably killing him that he hadn't been selected yet but he did a good job of hiding his disappointment.

My first game was a memorable experience. There must have been about fifty thousand East Germans packed into Dynamo's stadium and when we ran out onto the pitch it felt like the whole ground was vibrating. It felt almost unreal. Somewhere in the stands my family would be watching and it felt good to think about how proud they would be feeling me jog out onto the pitch.

It didn't feel quite so good five minutes into the match when Lokomotive's man-mountain of a centre back hit me with an elbow to the back of the head.

"This is my pitch son," he laughed as he jogged past my crumpled body. "Keep away from me or someone might get hurt."

Mr Muller had warned me that I would have to expect a dose of rough treatment from their experienced defenders but I had hoped there might be a honeymoon period of at least ten minutes. Now here I was, lying on the turf with my head throbbing with pain.

There had been a time when I would have been intimidated by the thought of getting clattered but now I was made of sterner stuff. Mr Muller had drummed it into me over and over again. Don't show any sign of weakness whatsoever. With this in mind, I waited for my chance for a little payback. It came shortly after as I chased the man-mountain towards the corner flag. He misjudged how close I was to him and took the time to turn rather casually on the ball. Before he knew what was happening, I hit him hard, taking the ball cleanly but dumping him onto the athletics track that surrounded the pitch in the process. That's one all I thought to myself as the physio came on to treat him.

It was a bit of a scrappy game really, and very short on entertainment for the fans, but for me it was special. Twenty minutes into the second half, the ball was played through to me from the half way line and I was away, with clear daylight between me and their defence. I took three or four touches before I was in shooting range and as I looked up, I saw the goalkeeper rushing out to narrow the angle. It may have been risky but I was full of youthful confidence and dug my foot underneath the ball and over his head. For an awful moment, I thought I had clipped the ball too far but, fortunately the ball struck the crossbar and bounced down over the line and into the net. The crowd erupted with joy and I was mobbed by my team-mates. It was to be the first goal of many for me that season and I should have fond memories of that day. I don't. It was the day I first realised who my club was really run by.

Chapter 9

Being a fresh-faced newcomer to the first team, I hadn't met with any of the officials who owned the club before. As far as I was concerned, Mr Muller was the man who ran affairs and there was no-one above him on the ladder. How blind I was back then! Anyway, after the match against Lokomotive, the squad were invited to celebrate with the Chairman and the rest of the board members at an upmarket hotel in East Berlin. The win had kept Dynamo four points clear at the top of the league and, according to our goalkeeper, the chairman liked to celebrate success with 'his boys' from time to time.

Although he hadn't played in the match, Toni had been allowed to attend the party too. We found ourselves sitting around a table with the other players, sipping at beers that we weren't old enough to be drinking yet. The atmosphere was pleasant enough but the rest of the team seemed a little subdued considering we had just increased our lead at the top of the league. I spent half an hour or so chatting to Toni about the match while the rest of the boys mainly kept to themselves. It was certainly no wild party that's for sure.

Eventually, we were told that the Chairman was on his way and that he would like to personally congratulate us on our victory. It wasn't long before Mr Muller guided him to where Toni and I were sitting. Apparently, he wanted to meet the young prospect who had won us the match.

"Karl," Mr Muller said, "this is Erich Meier, honorary club chairman of Dynamo.

I got up and shook hands with the tall, wiry man who stood

before me. He appeared to be in his mid to late forties with receding dark hair that was beginning to show speckles of grey. Dressed impeccably in a grey suit, he told me how impressed he'd been with my debut. Although he smiled as he spoke to me, I didn't feel any warmth behind his words.

"You did well today my boy," he said as he moved on to speak to the other players. "Just you make sure that you keep that standard of performance up. Do you hear me?"

I nodded politely but I remember being slightly unnerved by the way he said it. It seemed vaguely like a threat rather than a message of encouragement and I also couldn't help noticing the reaction of the other players as he stopped at the other tables. They seemed to shrink visibly in his presence. Our chairman must be a powerful man I thought to myself. I asked Toni what he thought. He'd been unusually quiet too.

"Not here Karl," he told me.

Like I said, it wasn't much of an evening. I got the impression that no-one really wanted to be there.

"Come on," I said to Toni after enduring two hours of tedium. "Let's make a move."

As I began to stand up, he gripped my arm and pulled me back into my seat.

"It wouldn't look good for us to be seen leaving so early," he said quietly. "Stick it out a while longer."

I started to open my mouth to argue with him but there was something in his eyes that told me not to. I left it, sat down, and we ended up staying into the small hours. On the way back to the dormitory we still shared with two others, I pressed Toni about the party.

"What was that all about tonight?" I said, a little anger flickering in my chest.

Toni took a glance over his shoulder before grabbing my arm and taking a sharp left into a children's playground that we'd often pass on our way home. At this time of night, it was completely deserted.

"What are you doing Toni?" I hissed. It was a bitterly cold night and I didn't see why we couldn't talk on the move. After all, we were only five minutes away from the dormitory.

"Shh! Karl," he said urgently, pressing a finger to his lips and taking another look around. He needn't worry about anyone else being about, I thought to myself. No-one else is stupid enough to be hanging around here in this weather.

"Karl," he said at last. "Do you know who Erich Meier is?"

"Of course I do – he's the club chairm..."

"No Karl," Toni interrupted. "Do you know who Erich Meier really is?"

I stood there open mouthed. What could he mean? Did the man have some sort of secret identity? Toni wasn't making any sense. I had a fleeting thought that the alcohol we had consumed had clouded his mind.

"Toni," I said, resting my hand on his shoulder, "you're being..."

"He's Stasi Karl. They all are. The Chairman, the other board members, probably even Mr Muller. The Stasi own the club. The Stasi own us Karl. Do you hear me? We belong to them. We keep our heads down and just get on with our football. Do you hear me Karl?"

Chapter 10

The Stasi. Of course I knew of them but I'd never really thought that they could be involved with a football club, let alone my own. I'd just got my head down and trained hard for the last few years. Politics didn't interest me and I never even considered who owned the club. I was very naive back them. Toni was too until his brother had filled him in about Dynamo Berlin. If he was going to play for them, then it was important he went in with his eyes open so to speak.

The Stasi were the East German secret police force and were hated throughout the country. The regime tasked them with eliminating any opposition to their rule and they were not averse to locking up, torturing or shooting dead those who didn't conform. This included any unfortunate soul who was foolish enough to attempt an escape to the West. I remembered them knocking on our door on a few occasions, asking questions about our family on the other side of the wall and enquiring who my mother and father would be voting for in the forthcoming elections. As if they had any choice.

Everyone feared the Stasi and their network of spies. They were rumoured to have a huge network of informers who would gather files and files of information on just about anyone, particularly those who they deemed likely to try and flee the country. The thought of somehow being part of their organisation made me feel extremely uncomfortable. That night, I decided I was going to leave Dynamo for good. At one point, I was going to pack my bags there and then, walk out of the door and never look back but Toni talked me out of it.

"We've worked too hard to just throw everything away," he said. "Why don't we both stick it out for the rest of this season, try and establish ourselves as regular first team players and then get a move to another club in the summer? Neither of us want to turn our back on football for good, do we Karl? Besides, we are football players, not politicians. We care about what happens on the pitch, not off it, don't we? Let's keep ourselves to ourselves and just focus on winning matches."

As usual, Toni made a powerful argument. I wasn't totally convinced but football was my whole life and I couldn't bear the thought of my career ending before it had even really begun. I agreed to stay for the rest of the season.

I may have been a little apprehensive about training the following Monday morning but to be honest nothing had changed and it didn't take me long to get back into the swing of things. Over the next three months, I remained in the first team and made a big contribution to Dynamo's success too, scoring eight goals in ten matches. With half the season gone, we were four points clear of our nearest rivals in the league. It felt good too, even more so when Toni began to establish himself in our midfield. We'd dreamed of this moment for years and I must admit that I began to forget about who owned the club. There was the odd after match party in which we would have to play up to being one of the chairman's 'boys' but it was a small price to pay for the sheer exhilaration of playing football as a professional. I even thought of reversing my decision to leave at the end of the season.

Then, early in the new year, things changed. After another good win in the league, we were due to play in the European cup against West German champions Bayern Munich. Although we were massive underdogs, the club was buzzing with excitement before such a big match. I was too. It didn't seem so long ago since Toni and I had watched Bundesliga teams play on TV using our rigged-up aerial and I wondered what Erich Meier would think if he knew that two of his star players had participated in such illegal practices.

Anyway, on the day of our final training session before travelling to Munich, there was a knock on my door. Toni had stayed at his parent's house the previous night and the two other boys that I shared the dormitory with had already left for an under 19's match that they were involved with. I was on my own, although I have to say that I often enjoyed a little solitude now and then. Toni may have been my best friend but as I've said before, his incessant chatter could be draining at times.

A little surprised, I answered the door to find a police officer standing there in front of me. I recognised the man too. He was often hanging about at the club fishing for information on behalf of the Communist party. All of the players tried their best to avoid him.

"You don't need to attend training today," he said politely enough, although there was an assurance in his voice that indicated to me that this wasn't up for discussion. "There are people who want to meet with you today. Important people."

I felt a lump form in my throat and a sickening feeling began to develop in the pit of my stomach.

"I can't miss training," I tried telling him. "We have a big game this week and Mr Muller will be livid if I don't turn up today. We're going over out tactical plan. Everyone's got to be there."

"I've already cleared it with Mr Muller," the policeman continued calmly. "Come on now Karl – we don't want to keep people waiting, do we?"

My voice croaking slightly, I tried a different tact.

"Can't we just sort things out here between us. I'm more than happy to talk with you but I really don't want to miss training today. You can understand where I'm coming from can't you?"

"I can Karl. Really, I can, but I think you need to understand where I'm coming from. I have my orders to bring you to a meeting today by whatever means necessary. Let's not make this unpleasant shall we."

I stood frozen to the spot, part of me wanting to push past him and make a run for it.

"Karl," the policeman continued, "if you have done nothing wrong, then you have nothing to fear today."

He looked right at me, almost as if he were trying to read my thoughts.

"You haven't done anything wrong have you Karl?"

I shook my head.

"Then come on. My car is outside. The sooner we get there the sooner we can get you back here. You never know – you might just make that tactics briefing."

Glancing at the firearm holstered at the policeman's side, I followed him from the room.

Chapter 11

Sitting in the back of the car, my mind began to whirl. A second police officer sat in the passenger seat but he didn't make any effort to introduce himself. It was clear that I was on my way to meet with members of the Stasi but what did they want with me? I'd done nothing that would have offended them. I wasn't planning to defect to the West. It didn't make sense. I wondered for a minute if my father had talked himself into trouble. He could be pretty scathing about the Stasi, especially if he'd drunk too much at the pub. He wouldn't be the first person to have one too many beers and spoken his mind to the wrong person. Informants were everywhere and it was difficult to know who to trust. I'd listened to my father rant about traitors who gave information to the Stasi. The dregs of our country he called them. It was awful really, worrying about so called friends or even family betraying you. It was no wonder that so many East Berliners were suspicious and paranoid all the time.

We finally arrived at a hotel near the city centre and I was led up the stairs to a suite on the top floor. I was terrified and it made me angry when I thought that this would be just the way they wanted it. They fed off people's fear and anxiety. Upon entering the room, I took a seat at the large wooden desk while the two police officers that had accompanied me on the journey over here stood beside the door. There they stayed, cold faced. I have to admit that my nerves had completely frayed by now. The waiting was killing me. I didn't know what to say or where to look. Come on, I thought to myself. Let's get whatever this is over with.

After what seemed an eternity, I heard footsteps in the corridor and the door swung open. In walked a tall man whose face I recognised immediately. It was none other than Dynamo's chairman Erich Meier.

"Good morning Karl," he said breezily, greeting me with one of his wide smiles. "Thank you very much for giving up your time today. I can't tell you how much I appreciate it. Can I get you some coffee perhaps?"

How should I react? Was it obvious that I was terrified or was I doing a good job of keeping my cool? I wasn't stupid. Meier may have put on a show of being thrilled to see me but he wanted something from me. Probably something I wouldn't like. I'd heard a few whispers from those brave enough to gossip about our honorary chairman and they didn't paint a pretty picture. Apparently, before the war, he'd had to flee Berlin after a warrant had been issued for his arrest with regards to the murder of two police captains. The story went that he had then taken refuge in the Soviet Union for the next decade before returning to occupied East Berlin and taking control of the secret police. If you believed what had been said, and I was undecided, it was he who'd personally overseen the construction of the Berlin wall, signing the orders to shoot all those trying to defect. As Meier took his seat on the opposite side of the desk, I wondered if this man could be capable of such murderous deeds. Outwardly, he was quite friendly but his eyes seemed cold and lifeless.

"Don't look so worried Karl. I don't bite. Well only my enemies anyway. We're not enemies are we Karl?"

"No Mr Meier, I don't believe so."

He laughed out loud and slapped the desk with his right hand.

"Of course, we could never be enemies Karl. You bring me such joy whenever I watch you play. Still so young too. I hope you can represent club Dynamo for the next fifteen years."

In spite of myself, my heart twitched as he watched my face for a reaction. A heavy silence lay between us.

"Why so quiet Karl? You're not thinking of leaving us are you?"

The smile from his face had evaporated now. Did he know that I had harboured thoughts of signing for another team come the end of the season?

"Players don't leave Dynamo Karl. They just don't."

Meier's gaze never left me as the words left his mouth. Was he threatening me? I tried to think of any other first team players who had left to join another club but I couldn't think of any. No-one who Dynamo still wanted anyway. Meier was right. Once you were at Dynamo, you stayed until you no longer served your purpose.

If I'd been a little wary about the reason for this unscheduled meeting, I didn't have to wait any longer for my fears to be confirmed.

"So Karl," Meier continued, "you've enjoyed your trips abroad so far have you?"

I remained silent, not entirely sure what he was getting at.

"Am I right in thinking you travelled with the squad for the matches in Denmark and Italy? France too I believe."

I nodded. "Yes Mr Meier," I was with the team for those games."

"That's good Karl. It's nice for young players such as you to experience playing against teams from a different country. I'm pleased. Very pleased.

"And while you were away in France Karl," he said, "do you remember any of your team-mates talking to a group of East Germans in your hotel bar?"

My heart sank. It was clear to me now. As it happens, I did remember one or two of the senior players chatting to some fellow countryman after our match in Paris. There were quite a few East Germans who had fled abroad and would often follow teams from their former homeland when they played in European competitions. No harm in that you might think and there hadn't seemed anything unusual on the night after our one-nil win in Paris. We'd had a few quiet drinks in the bar and a couple of the players had sat amongst a group of East German football fans in the far corner. It wasn't exactly a wild night out but I knew what Meier was reaching out for. He wanted information.

Anyone who had left East Germany was considered a threat by the Stasi. Those people now living a new life in the West were considered enemies of the state. I knew what Meier was thinking. Were there people who would attempt to entice Dynamo's players to defect? Perhaps feed them stories of a better way of life. The Stasi were constantly looking to snuff out any such plots in their infancy and dish out appropriate sanctions to those who were deemed to be ringleaders. Clearly, one of Meier's army of informants had reported back to him that Dynamo players were talking to people they shouldn't be.

For me, this was an impossible situation. You defied the Stasi at your peril but I didn't want to become one of their snitches either.

"Which players joined the East German traitors at their table?" Meier asked firmly. "Was it Becke or Gabler? Brehme perhaps?"

Although I sat perfectly still, inside I was squirming.

"Karl – don't look so worried. No harm will come to them. I promise you that. They will receive nothing more than a reprimand. A slap on the wrist and no more. However, you must understand the position I am in. We cannot simply keep allowing our best people to thrive elsewhere. All that we build here in East Germany gone to waste with others reaping the benefit from out hard work. It simply cannot be allowed."

No harm will come to them I thought. How can I be sure of that? Like everyone else, I'd heard the rumours and even if only half of them were true, I didn't want to land Becke, Gabler and Brehme in trouble. If the Stasi believed that they were planning to defect then they would do everything in their power to prevent this from happening. Who really knew what Meier was capable of?

Trying to compose myself and hide how uncomfortable I felt, I tried to play dumb.

"Mr Meier," I said, "please forgive me but I don't think I can be of any assistance to you today. I am still a young player and after I'd finished eating, I went straight to bed. I have no real interest in drinking beer or anything like that. In the short time that I was downstairs, I didn't see anything unusual."

Meier's dark eyes seemed to burrow into my face.

"Are things going well for you at Dynamo Karl?" he asked.

"Yes Mr Meier, I suppose they are."

"You enjoy playing for the team."

"Yes," I said. And it was true. I loved playing football for Dynamo. If I could just have forgotten about their link with the Stasi, I would happily have given my entire football career to them.

"Do you want to continue playing for Dynamo Karl?" he asked me.

"Of course," I answered.

"Then you will need to work with us Karl."

"Mr Meier, I've always given you all I have. I keep my head down and work hard for you."

"You do Karl. You do. But we're not talking about your qualities on the pitch are we?

It was out in the open now. The friendly charade was over and I was filled with dread. How could I look at myself in the mirror each morning if I was running back and forth to the Stasi, feeding them snippets of information about topics of conversation in the dressing room and particularly any talk of defection to the West.

I bit my lip and somehow forced the words out.

"I didn't see anything in Paris Mr Meier. Really, I didn't. The senior players don't talk with me much either. Please – I just want to play my football and steer clear of any trouble."

Meier sighed.

"Karl – you are either with us or against us. You must make up your mind. I will take it in good faith that you know nothing on this occasion but I hope I will not find out you have lied to me."

He shook my hand and smiled.

"We will be watching you Karl. Don't do anything that will displease me."

I stood on shaky legs and walked to the door.

"Oh and Karl," Meier said as we finally parted, "I trust that you will not say anything about this meeting to anyone – not to your friend Toni and especially not your family. We don't want them to get caught up in things that do not concern them. Family are important Karl and we shouldn't do anything that will cause them any discomfort. Do you understand what I am telling you Karl?"

I nodded.

Chapter 12

I was badly shaken from my meeting with Meier and for a while it affected my game. I missed a few chances over the next few games which cost us points in the title race. How could I be expected to concentrate on football when I was being asked to spy on my own team-mates? An awful thought occurred to me that if I'd been asked to supply information for the Stasi, then who else was within their clutches? Were my colleagues watching me? Which players could I trust? Was Mr Muller Stasi? Surely he couldn't be. I had too much respect for him to entertain that idea for long but all these thoughts raced around my head like a high-speed train, crashing against the inside of my skull. Like many people in East Germany, I now lived in a state of paranoia, constantly wondering if people were watching me. When I sat in the club canteen with Toni, I couldn't help wondering who was listening to our conversation. When I paid a visit to my parents, I feared that I had been followed. My life didn't feel like my own anymore. After drawing another blank against Dynamo Dresden in a league match, my confidence was at rock bottom and the following Monday at training Mr Muller called me into his office.

"Good morning Karl," he said stiffly, "I thought it would be best if I talked to you in person this morning. I hope you don't mind spending a few minutes with me before training this morning."

"No Mr Muller – I don't mind."

Although I looked up to the boss, I was still afraid of him too. Even if I did mind, there would be no way I would tell him so.

"Good Karl – good. Let's get down to business right away then. I'm not one to waste words."

I nodded a little apprehensively. He certainly wasn't one to let his thoughts go unheard. I'd sat through some of his half-time pep talks when he had yelled at us so ferociously that I thought he would burst. He was fair though, was Mr Muller. He could bark like an angry dog if he felt you needed a kick up the backside but he also understood his players well enough to know when they needed an arm round the shoulder too. I liked the man – all of the players liked him.

"Karl, you have done extremely well for me this season and I couldn't have asked for any more. However, I think you are running low on energy at the moment and I am leaving you out of the side for the next game."

Emotionless, I sat there stone-faced.

"Karl," he continued, "don't take this too hard. You are young and your time will come again soon. Of that I am certain. You simply have too much talent to waste in reserve team football."

He sat back in his chair waiting for a response from me. I offered him nothing.

"Karl," he said gently, breaking the silence. "Why don't you take some time off? You should spend some time with your family, rest up and come back here raring to go in a week's time. It'll be good for you."

I didn't know what to do or say. I suddenly felt exhausted, as if the weight on my shoulders was crushing all the strength out of my body. I was no use to anyone in this state and it was no surprise that I was being dropped.

"Thank you Mr Muller," I managed to utter. I'm grateful for the time off and I will redouble my efforts when I get back next week. I don't want to disappoint you."

"OK Karl," he said. "I'll see you next week. Remember don't let this get you down."

I think he was expecting me to take my cue to leave the office but something kept me in my chair. Could I trust him? Could I trust this man that I admired so much?

"Is there something else Karl?" he asked, a touch of surprise in his voice. He studied my face for a moment.

"What is bothering you Karl? You've not been right for a while now. Whatever you tell me will not leave the walls of this office."

I told him everything. I don't know why because there was that small part of me that thought he could be working for the Stasi too. I just couldn't keep it in anymore and I respected Mr Muller. I couldn't imagine him being told what to do by anyone – even the Stasi. Nothing intimidated him. When I was done talking, he sat back in his chair and puffed out his cheeks.

"Thank you for telling me about this Karl," he said. "Please don't burden anyone else with this information. Leave things with me for a while. Enjoy the time with your family and we shall see how the situation is on your return."

Chapter 13

Spending time at home brought some welcome relief from the pressure I'd been under at Dynamo. It was good to catch up with my parents and Heidi too. My little sister was growing up fast. Fourteen years old now, and blessed with the same sporting genes that I'd been passed on by my parents, she was becoming quite an athlete herself. During the week, I was able to witness this for myself as I went to watch her in the regional schools' annual championships. Well, Heidi was absolutely the star of the show. The 400m was her event which requires a mixture of speed and endurance. Two qualities my sister had in abundance. With her long legs and lean physique, she absolutely blew the rest of the girls away, opening up a gap of at least thirty metres to her nearest rival before crossing the line. She'd taken at least a second off the school record and although I was proud of her, I did have the feeling that I would eventually become the second most talented sportsperson of the two of us. That afternoon, we sat in the tiny space that was our kitchen as she told me how she was going to run in the Olympics one day.

"I'm going to have a gold medal hanging around my neck by the time I'm twenty Karl," she'd said and I had no doubt that she meant it too.

"Well don't forget about your older brother when you are the darling of the nation," I said. "Make sure you come and visit from time to time."

"Ha ha, alright, perhaps just for a little while though. I'll be very busy with my training and I wouldn't want you to distract me." I laughed. My little sister had developed a cheeky sense of humour.

"And how would I distract you may I ask?"

"You would bore me to death with your football, football, football. Who wants to talk about a game where men do nothing more than chase a ball around a field?"

"Not you obviously Heidi," I said, not rising to the bait. "You clearly have far more important things to do with your spare time – what with your circling a track endlessly until your legs can stand it no more."

She punched my arm gently. "Stop it with your teasing Karl. If you are not careful, I will not come and see you at all after I become champion."

"Alright, alright," I laughed. "You know that would break my heart. No more jokes about your running – I promise. I know how much it means to you."

We talked a little while longer before I made my way to the front door. I needed to take my daily run to maintain my fitness.

"Do you fancy joining me? I'll make sure I go easy on you," I said. "Of course, if you're tired after your competition..."

Before I'd even had a chance to finish my sentence, she was halfway out of the door. I had to work hard to make up ground on her and when I eventually did, I saw a smile form on her face.

"Still planning on taking it easy Karl," she said.

The time spent at home did me the world of good and for the first time in months, I felt free again. I'd made up my mind for certain this time that I'd leave Dynamo at the end of the season. I didn't even care which team I went to anymore as long as I could leave. Meier couldn't stop me. I'd quit football altogether rather than play another season for him. When I returned to Dynamo at the beginning of March, Mr Muller was waiting for me.

"Welcome back Karl. I hope you enjoyed your time at home and are feeling refreshed."

"Yes, thank you," I replied.

"And you are ready to play for me again?"

I hesitated for a moment and Muller picked up on this indecision right away.

"Everything is fine Karl. You can concentrate on your football. Make sure you perform on the pitch and they will not bother you. I have Meier's word."

I had so many questions rattling away inside my skull. Why were they letting me off the hook? What had the boss said to them? Could anyone trust Meier's word? Muller had chosen his words with care. Make sure you perform on the pitch and the Stasi won't bother you. Was there a veiled threat to me in there somewhere?

I think Muller could sense how I was feeling. One of his qualities as a manager had always been a good understanding of his players. What motivates them? Do they respond better to praise or criticism? What makes them tick?

"Meier is no fool Karl. You are an asset to him. If your mind is not focused, then you cannot do your best for Dynamo. Young, gifted players such as yourself are too valuable to simply throw onto the scrapheap. All I did was to remind him of this fact. Now you can get back to doing what you do best. I've pencilled you in to start up front on the weekend."

Muller began to talk with enthusiasm about his tactical plans for the game and I nodded and did a good job of feigning interest. However inside, I just felt numb. I never thought that I'd feel this way but football just didn't interest me anymore. Becoming a professional player was all I'd ever wanted but it had turned into a nightmare. I was just an asset to Dynamo – someone who could bring glory to the hated Stasi. The thought of scoring goals and winning trophies for them sickened me but I resolved to get my head down and play. Not for Meier of course but for myself. There were three months until the end of the season and if I played well there would be other clubs queuing up for my signature. Perhaps then I'd be free again.

Chapter 14

So, I was back in the first team and it wasn't long before I was scoring goals again. Only now, every time I struck the ball into the back of the net, I saw it as a step towards getting a transfer away from Dynamo and away from the clutches of the Stasi. If anything, I began to play with a greater intensity than before and my performances helped the team open up a seven-point lead at the top of the first division. However, after my encounters with the Stasi, I now saw each game through very different eyes. With each victory came nagging doubts. I remember the first game in which they surfaced. It was a home fixture against our closest rivals FC Magdeburg. Before we kicked off, I remember being consumed with tension as I felt sure it would be an almighty physical battle between the league's top two teams. It certainly had been earlier in the season but this time it was anything but.

From the moment the referee blew his whistle to begin the match, I was expecting their centre back to be all over me like a rash. He certainly had been every other time I'd faced him and I still had the scars to prove it after he had raked his studs down the back of my calf muscle. He was a big old lump (aren't all centre backs) and he liked to make sure you knew he was about. In other words, he would kick you up in the air at the first possible opportunity. In this particular game though, he seemed strangely subdued.

The game must have only been only five minutes old when Toni knocked a ball over the top for me to chase after. The pass was a good one but it left me a little wide of goal. I remember thinking that by the time I'd taken a touch, their centre back would have cleaned me out with a thumping tackle. With that in mind,

I thought my best option would be to strike the ball first time. Even though it was a narrow angle, I was hoping to angle the ball towards the far corner and possibly force their keeper to parry it out to one of my team-mates.

So, there I was bearing down on goal when I became aware that the centre back wasn't as close to me as I thought he was – as close as he should have been. In fact, there was clear daylight between us and my first thought was that he might have pulled up with some sort of muscle injury. In the end, I had time to take a touch, look up and roll the ball back across goal for Toni to blast it into the gaping net. It was all incredibly easy. Too easy for such a big game like this.

And that's how it was for the rest of the match really. Easy. We won three goals to nil without even playing at our best and I'd never been given so much space. Our fans were delighted and so was Mr Muller but I felt strangely uncomfortable. When I walked off the pitch at the final whistle, I went to shake hands with their centre back. He hadn't been his normal competitive self and had suffered a poor game.

"No hard feelings," I said.

He barely even acknowledged me and headed straight down the tunnel towards the dressing rooms. He didn't seem angry or upset but just cold and emotionless. It got me thinking. He'd made no glaringly obvious mistakes but I knew he hadn't been on his game today. I'd been given a yard more space than usual and been allowed to take a few more seconds on the ball. He hadn't even bothered to kick me either which was definitely unusual. If anything, he'd seemed completely disinterested, as if the result didn't matter. How could that be when there was so much at stake? What had changed since the last time we met? Had he simply played badly or had someone encouraged him to do so?

Over the next five games or so, these type of questions raced through my head. I began to question the soft free kicks given by a referee or a goal against us mysteriously ruled out for offside. Was the linesman correct to raise his flag? It was often quite difficult to tell when you're playing a full throttle but I became increasingly suspicious of officials. At important moments in games, decisions always seemed to go in our favour. After my experience with FC Magdeburg's centre back, I was also extremely wary of opposing players. All players can make mistakes of course but it really got me thinking when an opposition defender lunged in to give away a stupid penalty or when an underhit back-pass sent me clear on goal. The victories kept on racking up but for me there was nothing to celebrate. I'd make sure I'd look right into my opponent's eyes when we shook hands at the end of a game. "Did you give your best today?" I'd think to myself. "Did you play an honest match?" Too often, the answer would be no.

Anyway, the season was nearing its end. With a win in our next game, the club would become champions of East Germany for the fifth year in a row. Mr Muller, never usually one for getting carried away with success, seemed to have an extra spring in his step and Toni, even more so than normal, was almost bouncing off the walls with excitement, desperate to collect the first winner's medal of his senior career. What he couldn't understand, was why his best friend didn't share his enthusiasm. I wasn't the same anymore and he could sense something was up. On the eve of the match, he demanded to know what was on my mind.

"Alright Karl," he said, as we walked back to the dormitories after our final team briefing, "something is not right. You've not been yourself for a long time now."

"I'm fine Toni," I lied. "Just a little nervous about the game. That's all."

"Nonsense," he said, with a touch of anger creeping into his voice. "Have we not known each other long enough to be honest with each other? Don't lie to me Karl."

He was right of course. Toni was my best friend and I had

always been able to tell him anything. So what was stopping me? Why couldn't I talk to him? Perhaps I didn't want to draw him into my unhappiness. He'd been able to separate the fact that the Stasi owned the club from his own thrill of playing football for his hometown team. As he'd said on many occasions, he wasn't a politician, he was a sportsman. He didn't care what went on at boardroom level so long as he was allowed to get out on the pitch and play his football.

"Alright Toni – here goes," I said, "but I don't think you're going to like it.

"Fine Karl. Get whatever it is you want to say off your chest. Just make sure you're honest with me. That's all I ask."

"I'm going to leave Dynamo at the end of the season," I said, "And I'm sorry Toni, but this time you won't talk me out of it. I won't play for the Stasi any longer."

There I'd said it. I don't know why I was so afraid of telling Toni. Perhaps it was because I knew he didn't feel the same. There was no way Toni would leave Dynamo. He genuinely didn't care who ran the club as long as he was winning medals on the pitch. Seeing as Dynamo had won the East German first division for five years running, going anywhere else was a step down. It hurt me deeply that after this season, Toni and I would probably never line up as team-mates ever again.

"Karl, don't do anything rash. In the next week, we will be champions of East Germany. It doesn't get much better than that does it? This is what we've always dreamed of isn't it? What we've always worked so hard for. Don't throw it all away now Karl."

"There's nothing you can say that will make me change my mind Toni," I told him. "I can't do this anymore. My heart's not in it. I don't enjoy playing football these days – not here anyway. I need a fresh start Toni. Surely you can understand that."

For a while he was silent – for once completely lost for words.

"You're being foolish Karl," he said eventually. "You're going to look back one day and regret this decision. You really are. Dynamo have given us the opportunity of a life-time Karl. To play football for the best team in East Germany – lift trophies – travel to Europe. Who cares if we are owned by the Stasi so long as they don't interfere with our football? We've been blessed Karl and I'm truly sorry that you can't see that."

I could feel the anger beginning to creep through my veins. How could Toni be so blinkered?

"Have you ever wondered why we win the league every year Toni?" I shouted. "Sure, we have some good players, but does it still surprise you when we get a soft penalty late into a game or the opposition have a goal mysteriously disallowed for offside? Meier has the referees in his pocket Toni. They're on the Stasi's payroll. I'm convinced of it."

The venom in my voice shocked the both of us. I don't think I'd ever lost my temper to this degree and it wasn't even Toni that I was angry at. I think it was an outburst at the club itself and all that they represented.

"You're being paranoid Karl," Toni said after a long, heavy silence. "You truly are being paranoid."

"You're right Toni," I yelled, "You're absolutely right. I am paranoid. Why do you think I want to leave? I don't feel I can speak to anyone without worrying that they are reporting back to the Stasi. I can't shake the feeling that I'm being watched and I can't enjoy a victory on the pitch without the nagging feeling that we've been given a helping hand. So yes Toni – I probably am paranoid but if I am then Dynamo have made me that way."

Toni was angry now too. I could see his eyes narrowing and his face had reddened.

"We're getting nowhere here are we Karl? You are my best friend and always will be but I sense that there is nothing more to say to you today and I'm not going to allow your stupidity to ruin what I've worked for – what we've both worked for Karl. If you feel this way, perhaps you shouldn't play on Saturday. Why not just pack your bags now?"

With that, he turned away and left.

Later that evening, as I reflected on our argument, I had to concede that Toni had a point. Why should I play on Saturday? I was convinced I'd shown enough ability to earn a move to another club now and it would be easy enough to feign an injury and pull out of the side. Something stopped me from doing so. Maybe I didn't want to let Mr Muller down but I have to admit that there was a slightly selfish reason behind my decision to play too. I suppose I wanted to achieve something in my football career and as much as I despised Dynamo and what they represented, I thought that this could be the only chance I'd get to earn a league winner's medal. In my mind, I was playing for myself and not the club. I'd win my medal then I'd be done with Dynamo forever.

Chapter 15

Standing in the tunnel, on the day of the match, I should have been feeling a little nervous, a little on edge, a little exhilarated. The expectant Dynamo fans were making a heck of a racket, ready for another taste of success. The whole stadium was rocking but I felt no emotion whatsoever – no passion for the game at all. Having been granted a few days to spend at home with my family, I hadn't spoken to Toni since we'd argued. With time to reflect, I regretted the way we'd spoken to each other and hoped that we could clear the air before I left Dynamo in the summer. I glanced back at him as we lined up but he just stared right through me.

The game itself was a little edgy to begin with and a few of our players made silly mistakes. Unusually, Toni was off his game too and almost gifted their striker an opening goal after being caught in possession. In all honesty, it was a terrible game to watch and with fifteen minutes to go the score nil-nil. Perhaps unsurprisingly with all that was going on in my head at that time, I'd had a poor game myself, never really threatening to get on the score-sheet. It seemed like Dynamo would have to wait until the following week to secure the points required to lift the title. Then, with the minutes on the clock ticking away, Toni played the ball in behind the defence and I raced away from the two centre backs. I knew that my speed would help me get to the ball first and as usual I tried to form a picture in my head of how I would put the ball past the goalkeeper who was rushing from his area to confront me. The best option, I thought to myself would be to drop my shoulder and dribble the ball round him. This would allow me to roll the ball into an unguarded net.

Well, I sidestepped the keeper as planned but the speed at

which he'd rushed at me caught me a little by surprise and as I hurdled his despairing gloves, I landed a little awkwardly, my studs catching on the turf. To my embarrassment, I found myself stumbling desperately before losing control of the ball and falling to the ground. The crowd, as any partisan home fans do, howled for a penalty even though the goalkeeper clearly hadn't made any contact with me. Surely, the referee, who had enjoyed a clear view of the incident, wouldn't bow to this pressure. Not one of my team-mates had even bothered to appeal and had already trotted back to their positions, ready for a goal kick. Then I heard the roars. The referee was pointing to the spot and huge cheers rang out from the Dynamo supporters. Sprawled on the turf, I watched with a mixture of disbelief and horror while two of the opposition players protested vehemently. Another player stood over me, accusing me of a dive, his face contorted with rage. As I rose to my feet, he shoved me in my chest, prompting some of my own team-mates to run over and remonstrate with him.

Breaking free from the rapidly increasing scrum of angry players, I shouted to the referee and raised my hands in the air.

"No penalty," I said clearly. "The goalkeeper never touched me."

Well, from wanting to throttle me one minute, now I was the opposition's best friend. They began urging the referee to speak to me and confirm what I'd just said. For whatever reason, he didn't seem too keen to make his way towards me so I took matters into my own hands and approached him as he stood beside the penalty spot.

"No penalty," I repeated to him. "He didn't touch me – I stumbled.

To my astonishment, the referee continued to point to the spot and motioned me away from him. I was furious.

"Are you deaf?" I yelled. "He never touched me. No penalty."

Now it was my own team-mates who wanted to throttle me. Our big centre half literally dragged me away from the referee before I could argue any further and that was it as far as my protests were concerned. My face crimson, I watched as our captain struck the ball into the bottom corner of the net, all but securing the title. Dynamo would be champions again.

Sure enough, we held out for the last ten minutes or so. The league trophy was ours but I couldn't help wondering how many players and official Eric Meier had influenced to help us on the way. That evening, I had to endure a party held in the team's honour as our president paid tribute to the players and management staff. His boys were champions again.

Chapter 16

There were still three games of the season left, but having secured the league title already, they didn't carry any real meaning. I didn't actually play in any of them after picking up an ankle injury in training. I was quite relieved when the club doctor ruled me out for a period of four weeks as the thought of playing for Dynamo ever again filled me with disgust. Although I still had to report to the club for physiotherapy for an hour a day, Mr Muller allowed me to go home and spend some more time with my family. With the season now drawing to a close, all of the players would get the best part of a month off before reporting back for pre-season training in July.

So, when the day finally arrived for me to make my return to Dynamo, I was consumed with tension. The thought of telling Mr Muller that I wanted to play for a different club horrified me. No matter what I thought of the club itself, at that particular time, before things changed between us forever, I had absolute respect for the man who had given me my big chance in professional football. Knowing that I would disappoint him broke my heart. I spent a considerable amount of time running through possible ways of explaining the way I felt to Muller without accusing him of being part of the Stasi's conspiracy to rig Dynamo's results. In the end, I gave up. There were no words available for me to use. Sadly, I also began to wonder how close Mr Muller was to Erich Meier. Surely, he too, could see that our team were benefitting from many questionable refereeing decisions or opponents making a timely mistake. Was he part of this? I still didn't think so but with Dynamo, nothing surprised me. The sooner I got away from this club the better.

I was still fretting about facing Muller, when there was a sharp rap at the door. I have to admit that it caught everyone off guard as we weren't expecting anyone at this early hour. A little apprehensively, my father got up from his chair, walked the short distance to the entrance to our home, and revealed the visitor. It was a surprising and unwelcome one.

"Good morning," Erich Meier said confidently, striding into the room and shaking my father by the hand. "I don't believe we've met before. You must be my boy Karl's father. Your son is a splendid young man – very talented. You must be extremely proud of him."

With my throat beginning to tighten, I watched in horror as my father forced himself to return Meier's smile. Behind the Stasi chief, stood a menacing looking man who I'd seen around the club before. Wherever Meier was, you could guarantee his personal bodyguard wouldn't be far away. It occurred to me that I'd never seen him speak before – not a single word. Today was no different and he just lurked in the background, with his dark, soulless eyes. Rather like a shark's I thought to myself.

Over the last few weeks, I'd told my parents that I was planning to leave Dynamo. Of course, I'd remembered Meier's veiled threat about speaking to my family about the Stasi's involvement at Dynamo so I hadn't told them the full details of the football conspiracy I felt Meier was operating throughout the East German league. I'd just simply explained that I wasn't happy with the way the club was being run and that I didn't want to represent them on the pitch any longer. Knowing that Dynamo had just been crowned champions, they were extremely surprised but respected my decision. My parents had always left me to stand on my own two feet. "Let the boy make his own mistakes and learn from them," my father had always said to my mother, and they had, leaving me to get on with my football at Dynamo without any interference.

Seeing my father's rather awkward expression, Meier introduced himself further.

"Forgive me for the early visit this morning," he said smiling. "My name is Eric Meier, club chairman of Dynamo Berlin. Karl has become one of my boys this season. When I see him play football, I can't tell you good it makes me feel. The runs he makes, the goals he scores – your son will become the best player in East Germany one day. That, I can promise you."

Meier then turned his attention to me.

"And that's why I have come to surprise you this morning Karl. I am here to reward you for the success you have helped bring to Dynamo this year. He gave a slight nod to his bodyguard who stepped forward holding a small briefcase. He took out some sort of papers and placed them down on our small kitchen table.

"This is your new contract Karl. It's a little more money and the club will also put you on a shortlist to own a car. If you continue to perform well, then you will be given your own accommodation shortly".

This may not have seemed like a lot considering how wealthy footballers in the West were becoming but to a young East German it was a fortune. Wages were a bit of a taboo really. Once a month, a bespectacled man would arrive at the club with a suitcase full of money. Each player would then visit him individually to receive their wages. There would be absolutely no room for negotiation or argument. You took your money and that was that. No-one would ever dare talk about it or compare their earnings to another's.

I stared down at the contract on the table as Meier sat down at one of the empty chairs.

"Come now Karl," he said, tapping his hand on the surface. "Don't be shy. I have a pen in my pocket. Let's get this done and we can get you signed on for the next six years. You should be honoured you know. I don't normally give a player more than three years so I must rate you extremely highly."

I stood there motionless for a while. It occurred to me briefly how comfortable Meier was in my own home, dictating orders as if my family and I were visiting him and not the other way round. Six years I thought to myself – I wasn't sure if I could face another six hours at the club. I don't remember how long I stood there, almost frozen in my nightmare, but I became aware that my silence was becoming uncomfortable. My father, aware of my imminent plans to ask for a transfer, could sense my discomfort.

"You must excuse me Mr Meier, but I think in football matters such as this, you and Karl should have some space to discuss things without us being in the way."

If Meier could feel a certain awkwardness in the room, he didn't show it.

"Of course," he said, still smiling. "Thank you. I promise that this business of ours should not take very long and once again, please accept my sincere apologies for interrupting your morning."

So, my father ushered my mother and Heidi out of the house, explaining that they would take a morning stroll to the nearby woods.

"A bit of exercise will be good for my joints," my father said as he stood in the doorway. Giving me a final glance as if to confirm it was alright for him to leave, he waited for a moment. I gave the slightest of nods and watched as my family slipped out into the street. A firm hand on my shoulder brought my attention back to Eric Meier. I hadn't noticed Shark eyes lurking behind me and although his gesture wasn't particularly threatening, I knew that it would be foolish to resist him as he ushered me to the table.

Everyone knew how the Stasi operated through intimidation and fear and I was determined to show that I wasn't afraid. The whole culture in East Germany was geared towards conforming to authority. No-one seemed to be allowed to have a mind of their own or to make decisions for themselves. To me, the Stasi were the worst kind of bullies and I had to show them that they couldn't control me. I sat down on the chair and faced Meier while Shark eyes returned to his position at the rear of the room. I wanted so desperately to be bold and brave – to tell the both of them loud and clear that I was done with their corrupt club and that I would never return. However, finding the strength to say those words out loud to the chief of East Germany's secret police wasn't easy and despite my determination to show no fear, I could feel my hands shaking as I sat at the table.

"Sign at the bottom of the page please Karl," Meier said, handing me a pen. It was an order rather than a request and for a moment I weakened. I'll admit it. I was afraid of Meier and afraid of Shark eyes. In that moment, I was terrified and I could feel the blood pulsing through my veins as if would burst right through my skin.

"The bottom of the page Karl," Meier repeated with just the slightest hint of irritation. "What's wrong with you this morning boy?"

I closed my eyes and took a deep breath, physically puffing out my cheeks.

"No," I said at last, almost surprising myself when the word finally squeaked out.

The look on Meier's face gave nothing away but I was sure as commander in chief of the Stasi, he wasn't used to being refused, not least by some teenager who should be honoured that he'd been given a chance to play football for the biggest club in East Germany.

"What do you mean no?" he laughed. "No, you don't understand where to sign."

"I know where to sign," I replied softly. "I'm just not doing it Mr Meier. I don't want to play for Dynamo anymore I'm afraid. I appreciate the chance the club have given me but I will be leaving this summer. I've played my last game."

A huge weight had been lifted off my shoulders. Things were out in the open now and there was no turning back. I saw Shark eyes take the smallest of steps forward before Meier raised a hand to stop him in his tracks. Then there was silence, as he sat back in his chair as if contemplating his next move.

"Thank you for your honesty Karl. I'm pleased in a way as now we no longer have to lie to each other. That's a good thing isn't it Karl?"

I remained mute.

"I said that's a good thing isn't it Karl?" Meier repeated.

"I suppose it is Mr Meier," I replied, keeping my tone and manners as polite as possible. Of course, I wanted to leave the club but I also knew that it wasn't wise to aggravate the Stasi any further than I needed to.

"Do you know Karl, that in many ways, I admire you? There are not many people who have defied me over the years. It shows you have a bit of character about you. I honestly didn't think you had it in you. I really didn't."

He began smiling again.

"When my sources at the club told me what you were thinking, I couldn't bring myself to believe that you would be so ungrateful. Even after that ridiculous behaviour during your last game, I just couldn't see you actually going through with it."

As I sat there, I racked my brains for information. Who had told Meier that I wanted to leave? Had any of the players got wind of my plans? Had Mr Muller given me away? The thought horrified me but what if Toni had said something? He'd been so angry at me when we'd last spoken but surely he wouldn't have betrayed me like this.

"Don't worry Karl," Meier continued, interrupting my thoughts. I can be of a forgiving nature when it's in my best interests. It actually pleases me to think that a young boy like you can stand up for yourself when so many grown men wouldn't dare to. That's the type of spirit I want my football players to show. It's just a shame that I'm going to have to decline your request for a transfer. You are simply too important to the future of my club."

Becoming a little bolder, I bristled at Meier's arrogance in believing he could simply dismiss my request for a transfer.

"I'm sorry Mr Meier but I've made up my mind," I said. "I'm extremely grateful for the opportunity that Dynamo have given me but I just don't think we are a good fit anymore. I would never want to disrespect you in any way but you can't force me to play football for you. It would never work. An unhappy player just won't perform for the team and you know that as well as me. Please Mr Meier, I don't want any trouble and I'd like us to part on good terms if possible."

Meier's eyes began to narrow.

"You just don't understand do you Karl?" he said calmly but with a coldness that frightened the life out of me. "My people and I make the decisions in this country, not some boy who can play a reasonably good game of football. I was hoping things wouldn't become unpleasant between us but let me spell things out for you Karl so there will be no misunderstandings in future. You will continue to play for Dynamo until I deem your time is done. This will not ever be your decision Karl. It will be mine. Do you hear me? You will leave this club when you are no longer an asset to my team."

I listened as Meier told me exactly what would happen if I ever spoke about leaving the club again.

"And don't even think about setting out on the pitch and giving me some sort of half-hearted performance," he continued. My people will be watching you everywhere Karl. Everywhere. During matches, training, your home, we will be monitoring your behaviour Karl and I will decide whether you are giving me your best effort because if you don't then it will displease me. Do you know what will happen if you displease me Karl?"

I didn't answer. Even if I'd wanted to, my throat was now becoming too dry to speak.

"I said, do you know what will happen if you displease me Karl?" Meier repeated quietly.

"No Mr Meier," I managed to blurt out. "I don't."

"Well, let me describe it to you Karl but be assured that I didn't want it to come to this. You are one of my boys and I don't like to speak to you in this way. Do you hear me Karl?"

"Yes Mr Meier, I hear you."

"Firstly, let me say that you are finished with football if I ever hear of this nonsense about leaving Dynamo again. No other team in the country will dare take you on if I say you are damaged goods. Depending on how I feel about any further betrayal Karl, I may not just be content with ending your promising career but might ask one of my colleagues to ensure you have the physical scars to remind you of what happens to those who defy me. My colleague here would have no problems breaking those ankles of yours if I give him the go-ahead."

Feeling physically sick, I risked a glance at Shark eyes. He remained impassive.

"And then it's not just you who will be harmed by your disloyalty," Meier said, almost with a hint of sorrow.

"I will be forced to make your family suffer too. Citizens must have a clear message that we cannot tolerate any challenge to authority in this country."

"Please," I begged. Don't punish them for anything that I have done."

"But you haven't done anything have you Karl? Not yet anyway and if that remains the case, then your family need not worry about a thing. Your mother and father will not lose their jobs and I shall allow them to keep this small home of yours. If you get your head down and work very hard for me, perhaps I will choose not to find a convenient excuse to have your father taken to the Hohenschönhausen (the Stasi Prison) and interrogated. Believe me Karl, that is not where I would want anyone that I care about to end up. After six months of isolation, deprived of sleep in a cell so small that you can't even stand up, people will say anything to me

– even if there's no truth in it whatsoever.

Meier let that thought sit with me for a while before starting up again.

"Finally, and I truly feel awful about this Karl, but I have to mention your sister. Her name is Heidi isn't it."

My heart sank deeper and I felt tears burning in my eyes.

"I asked you a question Karl," Meier said and for the first time he raised his voice.

"Yes," I said while biting my lip so hard I felt a trickle of blood in my mouth. "You know it is."

"And I understand the girl is an incredibly talented athlete."

Head bowed, I nodded.

"Your family have good genes Karl. From what I hear, she dreams of running in the Olympics one day, and with the way she's going there is a good chance she will do."

"Don't hurt her Mr Meier. I promise you I'll do what you want," I told him. "I'll sign the contract right now but don't hurt Heidi."

"Pick up the pen Karl, there's a good boy," Meier instructed.

"And I'm no animal you know. I have no intention of any of my men taking a hammer to her ankles. Not unless I am provoked. No – that would be awful. I'm thinking of quite the opposite in fact. During the week, I will approach your father with the offer of a scholarship for Heidi. She will be invited to join our athletics academy and I can promise you that our specialist coaches will give her the best opportunity of reaching the Olympics one day. Do you hear that Karl? She will train here at the Dynamo sports complex. However, if you choose to make yourself an outcast at Dynamo then that girl will never represent her district in athletics let alone run for this country. Of this you can be sure Karl. I am a man of my word. Do you want to be the one to destroy your sister's dream? She would hate you forever more, would she not?"

I was beaten. With trembling fingers, I signed the contract in front of me. I belonged to Dynamo now. They owned me and there was nothing I could do about it. I'd seen the full evil face of the Stasi at last and who knows what they were capable of. From now on, I wouldn't play football with any freedom or joy. I'd run myself into the ground to make sure that I was seen to be giving Meier my best. I'd have to or my family would suffer the consequences. As Meier left, with Shark eyes following closely behind, he turned towards me.

"Remember that this stays between us now – don't draw any of your friends and family into this. And Karl," he said, "it really hurts me to have to speak to you like this. Please don't disappoint me in the future."

Chapter 17

My father is not an idiot. He knew Meier and Shark eyes were Stasi.

"They stand out like a sore thumb," he told me. "I'd heard lots of rumours about Dynamo being the Stasi's team but I don't think I really believed it."

Then he was serious for a moment.

"You're not in trouble are you Karl?" he asked. "I can't imagine they took kindly to your decision to leave."

"No," I admitted, they didn't but things are going to be alright now Dad. We've ironed out our differences and I've signed the contract."

My father frowned ever so slightly. I could feel his anxiety.

"Are you sure?" he asked. "It doesn't pay to make enemies of the Stasi Karl. I've heard about the way they operate. They could make things extremely uncomfortable for you."

"Don't worry Dad – I'll be fine."

My father's face went pale.

"Look Karl," they won't just make life uncomfortable for you if you cross them. Your mother and I can't afford to lose our jobs Karl – you understand that don't you?"

"Yes Dad, I know. Things will be fine from now on."

My father, not usually one for any physical contact, draped an arm around my shoulder.

"I'm really proud of you Karl – I want you to know that. I can see why you wanted to leave Dynamo but you're not accountable for who owns the club. You just focus on playing football son – do you hear me? Start enjoying it again and don't concern yourself with what goes on off the pitch. It's not your problem Karl. Sport and politics should be kept separate."

"I know Dad," I said. "You sound just like Toni but you're both right. From now on, I'm just going to get on with my football."

"Good son," he replied. "It's for the best. It really is."

So, in the end, I had no choice but to return to Dynamo for pre-season. It took every ounce of my strength to put on a good show for everybody on my first day back at training, running until my lungs were fit to burst, feigning enthusiasm at every opportunity and even forcing a smile for the team photograph. I knew that the Stasi would be watching my every move from now on and I couldn't afford to slip up. In fact, the only thing I couldn't bring myself to fake was my friendship with Toni. I was still angry with him and he probably felt the same way about me. I did my best to avoid him so as soon as our final fitness session was over, I headed off home as quickly as possible.

Under the conditions of the contract that I'd been coerced into signing, the club had provided me with my own apartment so thankfully I wouldn't have to share a dormitory room with Toni or any of the other boys any longer. Having said that, I didn't enjoy living on my own. I was totally convinced that the Stasi had the rooms of my apartment bugged so they could listen to any conversations that I had with my visitors and spent large amounts of time checking for listening devices. Either there weren't any or the Stasi were more skilled in hiding them than I was at finding them.

That evening, as I sat at home resting my aching legs, I heard a knock at my door. It was Toni.

"May I come in Karl?" he asked.

I nodded, showed him into the front room of my apartment and poured us both a drink.

"Look Karl," Toni began, "I'm sorry about the way we left things. I still don't agree with you but I'm truly sorry that it caused us to argue."

I didn't respond immediately. I just listened.

"I'm glad that you changed your mind Karl," he continued. "I'm thrilled that you're staying at Dynamo. You're my oldest friend and I didn't want to lose you. I think that's why I got so angry with you for wanting to leave."

I remained quiet.

"Anyway – Whatever convinced you to stay here, I'm grateful. That's all I wanted to say."

If only he knew what it took to convince me I thought to myself. If only he knew how appalling a man Eric Meier was. I wanted to tell him everything but I just couldn't. Explaining the threats that had been made to my family would only draw Toni into the situation as Meier had promised. That wouldn't be fair to him so I kept my mouth shut. If my suspicions were correct, the Stasi could be listening to this very conversation anyway.

"Thanks for hearing me out Karl," Toni said. "I won't keep you any longer – just wanted to get things off my chest that's all."

He got up to leave but I stopped him in his tracks.

"Thank you for coming Toni. I mean that," I said and I shook his hand. "And I'm sorry too. I was out of line losing my temper with you. You're my best friend and always will be. Let's not argue any further."

Looking relieved, Toni nodded and smiled.

"See you at training tomorrow," he said as he left.

"Right – see you tomorrow Toni," I replied and as I watched him I realised how lonely it was having the weight of the world on your shoulders and not being able to confide in your friends and family.

Chapter 18

Over the following two years, I helped Dynamo continue racking up the trophies and I gave Erich Meier what he wanted. With that little bit more maturity, I improved my game further but my love for the game was now lost forever. I managed to maintain a high level of performance because I knew that I had to. Not a day would pass without Meier's threat to my family rattling around inside my head. It was a suffocating feeling.

It was nice to have a family member close by though. My sister Heidi was given the scholarship that Meier had promised and now lived in the block of dormitories that I'd once stayed in. At first, I'd been horrified at the thought of Heidi representing Dynamo but I also had to recognise that she would never realise her Olympic dream if she didn't begin training with the best coaches and Dynamo had those in abundance. Their athletes were becoming the pride of the nation and many had already won medals on the world stage. Besides, Heidi was young and innocent and was only focused on doing well in her chosen sport. She didn't know much about the Stasi and I felt it was best that she never did. Of course, athletics was completely different to football anyway and the way Heidi was going she would be competing on the world stage at some point in the next three to four years. Eric Meier may be able to influence East German football but his influence did not spread to other countries. I'd noticed how our referees in European competitions didn't give us the same preferential treatment we enjoyed in our domestic league. Even a powerful man such as Eric Meier couldn't just rig an Olympic final.

Heidi and I would often end up training at the same time. I

could see her racing around the athletics track while I took part in shooting practice. At least twice a week, we would end up meeting up and having lunch together. I didn't really take any enjoyment out of telling her about how my football was going so I was quite content to sit back and let her tell me how her times were improving rapidly and how her coaches were really happy with her progress. Apparently, they would soon be moving her up the performance ladder, whatever that meant. It was great to see the enthusiasm Heidi had for her chosen sport and it pleased me that she had not come across the sinister side of the Stasi.

During this period, the wall that divided both our city and our nation changed too. It was now even tougher to cross with an eleven-foot, ten-inch concrete structure with steel tubing over the top. There was also now a signal fence that would trip an alarm, watchtowers, spotlights, strips of 5-inch spikes, minefields and trenches before you even got to stand beside the actual wall. Yet still, many East Germans were desperate enough to make an escape attempt and defect to the West. As I said before, you could never be sure exactly which stories were rumours and which were true but there were so many of them that they surely couldn't all be fantasy. One story that I heard whispered about on many occasions, concerned a young man named Ingo who navigated a fence, a tripwire and a minefield before sailing across the River Elbe on a padded mattress and into West Germany. Even more amazingly, and surely they couldn't be true this time, were whispers that Ingo's brother had plotted an equally daring escape. If you were to believe the tale, his brother Holger had joined him in West Berlin by firing a wire cable over the wall from a high-rise building and riding a zip-wire to freedom. It didn't sit well with the Stasi if you were caught spreading such rumours but many people were prepared to take that risk.

For me, even thinking about defecting to the West was frightening. Erich Meier had made it clear that my family would suffer if I did anything to displease him and I couldn't do anything that would jeopardise them. So, it was with a mixture of shock, fear and excitement that I received a request from one of my fellow Dynamo players to help him defect. Emil Fischer had only been with Dynamo for six months having being transferred from Dresden in the close season but I could tell he was different right from the first time he introduced himself to me. You see, Emil was not your typical East German footballer in that he was a bit unpredictable – maybe even a bit of a maverick when compared to the rest of us who wouldn't dare to challenge the way the team was run. Unlike me, Emil absolutely loved his football though. He played each game as if it were his last, and in a country where any sort of individualism was frowned upon, his skill and flair made him extremely popular with the Dynamo supporters. He was a terrific player to watch and that probably gave him some leeway with Erich Meier when it came to turning a blind eye to some of his antics on the field, because as jovial and likeable a character Emil was off the pitch, he could be extremely argumentative and difficult on it. Mr Muller used to give each player specific instructions that they were meant to follow to the letter but they were often wasted on Emil. He had no time for complicated tactical instructions and like he often said himself, he didn't know what on earth he was going to do until the ball arrived at his feet. At times, he could be having an absolutely awful game, incurring the wrath of Mr Muller, before he would pop up with one moment of magic to win us the game. Emil won us many points with his goals but I don't think Mr Muller would have tolerated him if his transfer hadn't been personally organised by Erich Meier, who was a big fan of his style of play. The only problem was that Emil hadn't ever wanted to leave Dresden. He'd been forced into the move against his will and he was still angry about it. Eric Meier had past form with this type of manoeuvre and talented players from Dresden were often ordered by the state to up sticks and move to Dynamo Berlin. This didn't sit too well with Emil.

Apart from Mr Muller perhaps, everyone liked Emil and he and I got on particularly well. So well in fact, that he asked for my help one afternoon after training. His apartment wasn't far from my own and we often made the short walk home together. When he was sure no prying eyes were watching us, he came right out with what he had planned. From previous conversations I knew he had no love for Erich Meier and his secret police but what Emil told me that morning shocked and frightened me in equal measures.

"Can I trust you with my life Karl?" he asked as we stopped in the alley behind his apartment block.

At first I thought he was kidding around as usual but something in his manner was different from normal and it made me realise that he was serious.

"Of course Emil," I said. "What's wrong?"

"This is not the life for me Karl," he continued.

"What do you mean?"

"I don't feel free here Karl," he said. "I'm not going to be part of the Stasi's game. I'm going to leave as soon as possible."

I paused for a moment. Should I warn him of what I'd already experienced at the hands of Meier? Did he know what the Stasi were capable of?

"I'm not sure it's that easy Emil," I said. "I don't think they'll just allow you to go to another team."

"I don't just mean that I'm going to leave Dynamo," he said, "I'm going to leave the country and I'm never going to return."

This stopped me in my tracks. To defect to the West was the most treacherous of all crimes and the Stasi would go to any lengths to avoid this happening. Even talking about it would land you in prison, let alone attempting it. And that was just for normal citizens. High-profile sportsmen like us were important to try and maintain national pride and instil confidence in the government. Our movements were monitored extremely closely and potential defectors were left in no doubt about the consequences of fleeing. For a moment, a horrible thought struck me. Was Emil a Stasi informant? Had Meier tasked him with trying to sound out my thoughts about defection? I hated myself for thinking that way but I couldn't help it. I'd got to know Emil pretty well over the last six months and I was sure he was being sincere but I thought it best to remain guarded.

"I know what you're thinking Karl," Emil said, breaking the silence. "I'd probably think that way too but you're wrong – I'm not Stasi."

I stood in silence, still half in shock.

"I'm not Karl," he repeated, gripping my jacket as if to emphasise the point. "I can't stand those people and I want out. I think you do too if you're honest with yourself. I'm pretty sure you've had your fill of playing matches in which the result has already been decided. I've seen how empty you look after a win Karl. Tell me you don't feel the same as me."

I nodded, still afraid to say the words out loud, still half-thinking that Emil was carrying a wire somewhere on his person.

Our forthcoming European tie was against St Etienne. We'd qualified for the quarter finals of the European cup against the French champions. Emil had made his mind up.

"I'm going to make a break for it the night before the St Etienne match," he declared. "Then I'm going to walk into the West German embassy and claim asylum. Come with me Karl. A life in the West will be so much better for both of us. I know of many European teams who would snap us up and pay us a lot of money. Who knows Karl? You might find your love for football again."

My God, I thought. He's serious. He's really going to go through with this. I felt a surge of exhilaration followed by a crushing disappointment. There was no way I could leave. Even if I found the nerve to attempt to defect then I couldn't leave my family at the mercy of the Stasi.

"I can't Emil," I said sorrowfully. I just can't do it. I'm sorry."

I didn't want to say anymore really. What could I do? I was trapped.

"It's OK Karl," Emil said after a lengthy pause. "I get it. They'll get to your family if you don't do as they say. They said us much to me before my mother died last month. I haven't seen my father since I was three. I have no family now which is very sad but it also means there is nothing to hold over me either. For you, this is not the case, so I understand Karl – I really do. All I ask of you is one thing. If you won't come with me then I need you to help me."

Chapter 19

I have to admit that the thought of helping Emil escape thrilled me. I might not be able to leave Dynamo myself but I enjoyed the thought of Emil defecting to the West immensely. I knew it would be humiliating for Erich Meier and anything that caused him any sort of discomfort was great news for me. Emil had explained to me how I could assist him with his escape without drawing any suspicion towards myself and I was ninety per cent certain that I would do it. I hadn't given him my final word yet but I'd promised him a decision in the next few days.

Understandably, all the fear and excitement left me a little on edge, especially as I knew there were Stasi agents watching me closely. Toni, who had always been able to tell if something was wrong, picked up on my change of mood quickly. After calling round one evening, he asked me straight out what was bothering me.

"Alright Karl," he said, "I know by now when something is troubling you. I thought things between you and the club were good now. I was made up when you decided to stay last summer and I'd hate to think that you've had second thoughts."

I kept quiet. I wanted to tell Toni about Emil's plans to defect but I didn't dare say a word. I couldn't draw Toni into any of this. Like he'd always said, he was happy at Dynamo – happy to play his football and happy to keep racking up the trophies. Why would he want to leave? He was living the life that he'd always wanted. Still, I hated not being able to confide in him. He'd always been there for me since we were young kids and over the last year or so our friendship had drifted. After putting the angry words of last summer behind us, we still got on well but I also realised that things had changed forever. The secrets that I carried with me could not be shared with anyone I cared about and that was the cruellest thing. The very people I trusted the most were the ones that I couldn't talk to.

"Come on Karl," Toni urged again, "I know that all is not well with you at the moment. You might be able to hide it from the others but not from me. Come on Karl. You've always been able to tell me anything. Why not get things off your chest? It might even make you feel better."

I rubbed my fingers against my temple.

"Do you ever think about what life would be like in the West Toni?" I asked.

His eyes widened a little and I saw something I'd never seen in Toni before. He was afraid. Almost immediately, he recovered his composure but I'd seen that fear alright.

"You shouldn't speak like that Karl," he replied. "We have plenty to be grateful for what we have here. We play football for the best team in East Germany. We have our own apartments and a car too. That's more than most people have. What else do we need Karl? Really – what else do we need? I have no desire for more wealth Karl and I'd be surprised if you do."

"I don't Toni. I have no desire to be rich either but it's not just about that is it?"

"I don't know Karl. I just want to play football. Please don't speak about things like this. If you even think about leaving the country, you would be making yourself a criminal. Do you understand that Karl? It wouldn't just be you that suffered either Karl. Think about your parents. Think about Heidi."

I shook my head. "Don't worry Toni. I won't be going anywhere. Even if it was what I wanted, I couldn't leave my family. I couldn't do that to them."

I could almost see the relief wash over Toni.

"Good Karl. That's good. Then why the foolish talk?"

I rubbed my temple again. This wasn't really a conversation I wanted to be having. I could sense Toni's mind whirring too and began to wish I'd never said a word.

"It's one of the others isn't it," he said suddenly. "One of the others is thinking of defecting."

I should have dismissed it straight away but I've never been a good liar. The split second or two that I hesitated for were enough to confirm Toni's suspicions.

"You be careful Karl," Toni said softly. "Don't get mixed up in anything that could cost you. You be careful," he repeated. "Do you hear me Karl? Don't do anything stupid."

Thankfully, later Toni seemed to relax and forget about the awkward conversation we'd shared earlier. To my relief, he left the subject alone and we chatted about other things for a while – family, football – even girls. He was on good form too, talking away at high speed as usual. We ended up opening a few beers and reminiscing about our time growing up together, sharing funny stories about scrapes we'd gotten into, managers we'd driven crazy and of course, recalling many excellent goals we'd scored over the years. It was a good evening and when Toni finally left, I realised that I hadn't laughed this much in years.

Chapter 20

As the match against St Etienne drew closer, I was a nervous wreck. Each day, I'd see Emil at training and I could barely look him in the eye. I so desperately wanted to tell him that I'd help him in any way possible but I couldn't find it within myself to do so. I have to admit that I was afraid and I hated myself for being so cowardly. I knew that's exactly what the Stasi would have wanted. Consumed by paranoia, for two days, I didn't even speak to Emil. For all I knew, and I certainly had my suspicions, some of my team-mates were on the Stasi payroll and would be watching my every move.

When I returned to my apartment each evening, I'd find it hard to get off to sleep, and when I eventually did, my dreams were full of the most dreadful images. I pictured my father being pushed roughly into one of the Stasi's cars, my mother and sister being thrown out of our house and Emil being gunned down as he made his break for freedom. Each morning, I'd feel physically sick and playing football was the last thing that I felt like doing. Finally, on the day before the match, I made up my mind. When training was over, I sat opposite Emil in the changing rooms. Pulling off my muddy boots, I caught his eye for the briefest moment and gave the slightest of nods.

Conscious that we shouldn't be seen talking together, we barely spoke during training. Emil had made it clear that once he had defected, the Stasi would instantly be looking to see if there had been any accomplices. Who'd he been talking to recently? Did anyone know of his plans? He didn't want any trouble to come my way. So, like I said, Emil barely said a word to me in the days leading up to the cup match. It left me wondering what he had in mind for me. How was I going to help him escape? Then, when walking off the pitch as Mr Muller brought the training session to a close, Emil jogged past me slowly. He uttered just four words.

"Your bag," he said quietly, "side pocket."

I'm sure it only took five minutes or so for me to shower, change and leave the stadium but the time really seemed to drag. Of course, I was in a desperate rush to get back home and open my bag but I was very aware that I couldn't show my heightened sense of anxiety. I had to remain calm. Eventually reaching the relative safety of my apartment, half expecting a dozen Stasi officers to be waiting for me inside, I checked inside the side pocket of my sports bag. Breathless with a concoction of exhilaration and fear, my trembling fingers rummaged around inside until I found the note. Emil had it all planned out. Before the match in St Etienne, the team would be staying overnight in a hotel before playing the following day. Naturally, the squad would be accompanied by around twenty or so faceless men, who never took their eyes off the players so it wouldn't be easy for Emil to simply slip away. In his note, he explained what needed to be done.

If my sleep had been restless during the last week, that night, I didn't even bother retiring to bed. My head was pounding almost as if all the thoughts racing through my mind were ricocheting off the insides of my skull. I wondered how Emil must be feeling. I couldn't imagine that he felt as bad as I did – and he was the one defecting. So, it must have been just after five in the morning when I heard the car pull up outside. To my surprise, I saw Mr Muller's large frame getting out of the vehicle. Immediately, I was alert. Muller had always been pretty straight with me but I wasn't sure how closely he worked with the Stasi. He'd never once visited my apartment so why now of all days. It sent alarm bells off in my head. I felt a slight sense of relief that I'd had the sense to destroy Emil's note.

"I'd like you to come with me Karl," he said. "There's someone I'd like you to meet.

When I didn't answer immediately he sensed my discomfort. "I'm not Stasi Karl," he said. "I come here today in friendship. Please trust me. I need to speak to you about your sister. Come with me Karl."

Chapter 21

We travelled in silence across the city, Muller's dark eyes never leaving the road. As we drove towards the outskirts of the city, my mind was racing. Where were we going? Who was I being taken to meet? What did Muller want with Heidi? He'd told me he'd come in friendship but I still had my doubts. A small part of me worried that this journey wasn't going to end well.

"Can you tell me where we're going please Mr Muller?" I asked quietly.

"We'll be there soon Karl," he replied, "It'll all be clear then.

This being the early hours of the morning, the roads were deathly quiet. The sun was just beginning to rise and the sky was gradually turning a brilliant blue. From my seat, I watched long shadows stretch themselves across the road ahead. I decided I'd made a mistake getting in the car with Muller. Something didn't seem right and I began thinking of my next move. Could I jump from the moving car perhaps? I'd be able to outrun Muller easily – of that there was no doubt. But what about Heidi? Why had Muller mentioned her? Was she in trouble?

I was buried so deep within my thoughts that I hadn't even noticed we'd stopped outside a small house. Muller got out of the car first, walked slowly over to the front window and gave it a soft rap. A few moments later, the door opened and he slipped inside, nodding to me to show he wanted me to follow. Not sure what to expect, perhaps used to obeying Muller's commands, I got out of the car on shaky legs.

The front room reminded me of my parents' home. Same kitchen doubling up as bathroom, same cramped living conditions.

As I entered, Muller was sat at a table alongside a young teenage girl. She was probably no more than a couple of years older than Heidi and even resembled her in terms of her physical appearance with her long dark hair and brown eyes. I couldn't think why but to me she seemed distant and withdrawn – quite the opposite of my sister. It was if someone had drained the life right out of her.

"Sit down Karl," Muller said with a touch of sadness. "I'd like you to meet my granddaughter Hanna. "We have a lot to talk about."

A little stunned, I took my seat at the table, not entirely sure what to expect.

"Do you know Karl, that Dynamo have been my club for as long as I can remember? I was there right at the start, when we began to build the club, way before the Stasi got involved. Those were the best days of my life Karl – the very best. It's a wonderful thing to be able to build a football club you know – finding talented young players like you and then helping them fulfil their potential."

I stared back at Muller blankly, wondering where he was going with this.

"The Stasi and I have always had a marriage of convenience," Muller continued. "It is to my shame that I've turned a blind eye to some of their wrongdoings so long as I have been able to run the playing side of the club without interference. I suppose I've been selfish in a way. I couldn't bear the thought of giving up on the hard work that I'd put into building Dynamo into a proper team so Meier and I came to an unspoken agreement. He wouldn't question my decisions on the football side of things if I didn't raise any eyebrows with regards to the way he ran the club away from the pitch. I know that this was the wrong thing to do but in a funny way I thought that I at least had Meier's respect and could talk him out of making any rash decisions."

He'd caught me off guard. Why was he telling me this on today of all days? Why now?

"Mr Muller," I said, looking him directly in the eye, "What do you want from me? Why have you brought me here?"

Muller sat back in his chair and puffed out his cheeks. To my surprise, I thought that I could see tears in his eyes.

"Hanna here," he said, gesturing towards the young girl, "shares your sister's dreams of running in the Olympics one day. At least she did once. She's a little older than Heidi but until recently Hanna was also part of Club Dynamo's athletics programme. The best two hundred metre runner of her age in the whole of East Germany too. That's our Hanna. The world at her feet."

Muller took another deep breath before reaching out across the table and gripping hold of his granddaughter's hand. He tried to continue speaking but the words seemed to choke in his mouth.

"It's alright Grandpa," Hanna said quietly. "It's alright. Why don't you make us all a drink?"

When Muller hesitated, she tapped his hand warmly and he rose from his seat and busied himself in the small kitchen area. I was left alone with Hanna.

"I was thirteen years old when I began training full time with Club Dynamo," she told me. She was extremely calm but I could hear the pain in her voice.

"It was the best day of my life. I'm sure you can relate to this Karl. It was all I'd ever wanted. My stepping stone to the Olympic games and a gold medal hanging around my neck. You've probably heard your sister tell you the same story. For me, there's no better feeling than crossing the finishing line in first place and for my first three years at the club, I was given every opportunity to do just that. Having full time coaches and doctors available to advise me and influence my training helped me make rapid progress. I won a lot of races and as the months passed my personal bests would keep improving."

I felt Muller place a glass of juice on the table beside me as he returned to his seat. He remained silent though.

"I was having the time of my life," Hanna continued. "Living in a school that allowed me to do all this sport and not just writing and arithmetic. The sporting festivals that I took part in were amazing and when I came home with silver from the Spartacus games, I was almost bursting with pride. Going abroad at such a young age was a fantastic experience too. I went to Italy when I was just fourteen. In our country, how many teenagers can say that? There was the food too. Bananas, oranges – as you know, not everyone has this type of privilege."

She stopped talking for a moment, half smiling, perhaps enjoying looking back on what had clearly been happier times. Her tone soon changed.

"Everything changed for me the day I was moved to the senior athletics squad at Dynamo. At first, I was incredibly excited as I believed it was the next natural step towards achieving my goals. Then I was given the blue pills for the first time."

She stopped talking for a moment as if unwilling to talk further about the subject. Blinking back tears, she stroked her fingers across the centre of her temple. Muller rose from his chair to comfort her but she stopped him in his tracks.

"I'm alright," she said. "I'm alright." She took a small sip from her glass and rested both of her hands on the table.

"When I was handed the pills for the first time, I didn't really question what they were. The club doctor just told me they were vitamins that would support my training. Vitamin C, vitamin B, calcium, magnesium – that sort of thing. We'd usually take them after a really punishing training session. To be honest, most of my training had become pretty intense and although I was still committed to making the step up to becoming a world class athlete, I have to admit that I no longer felt the same sense of joy that I had experienced when first arriving at Dynamo. My days were just so busy with school, training, school, training again. I've never been afraid of hard work but it was becoming exhausting both physically and mentally. Free time became a thing of the past and the coaches grew stricter and stricter with us all. If you weren't wearing your hat, you were punished. If you didn't have your thermal vest on you were punished. If you were caught eating ice-cream in public, you were punished. The pressure was incessant and it was impossible to relax."

Hanna took another sip of juice but her gaze never left me.

"The pills kept coming too. I actually heard one of the other girls ask what they were needed for but she was put down with some rather nasty remarks. After that, no-one else made any sort of comment whatsoever. In fact, it was made clear to us that it was completely forbidden to even talk about the pills at all – not even with each other. They meant it too and I felt as if I was being watched constantly. All the secrecy and having to be wary of what I would say to the other girls was very unsettling to say the least. Like I said earlier, all of the joy I had for my sport seemed to have evaporated and everything was much more demanding and business like. I may not have liked it but I told myself these were the sacrifices that I would have to make if I were to become an Olympian one day.

Anyway, whatever was in the pills, and at the time I had no idea, it made me feel much, much stronger. I found myself able to train with greater intensity and for longer periods of time. Recovery was important too. Whereas in the past, my muscles had ached for days after a tough training session, now my body seemed to be prepared for another punishing workout in next to no time. I felt my body beginning to change a little too. My legs, which had always been incredibly skinny, were starting to thicken out and my shoulders were beginning to become strong and powerful. All the while, my times began to get quicker and quicker. Our head coach told me that if I carried on with the same rate of progress, I would be a certainty to make the Olympic squad. It was all I had ever wanted, and I should have been delighted, but I wasn't. I'd never felt so miserable in all my life. Then, last week, my mother found the pills in my sports bag."

Muller stood up from his chair and put his arm around his granddaughter.

"My daughter had no idea what the pills were for," he said but she was curious, and if truth be told, a little uncomfortable about discovering them in Hanna's bag. She put them back and didn't mention them. Instead, she called me to ask my advice. At first, I wasn't sure what to make of things either – probably just vitamins I told her, and although I believed this, I was left with just the smallest amount of nagging doubt. I began to do some digging. Of course, being the manager of Dynamo Berlin for so long meant that I could call upon a few different contacts for information. One of the medical staff at the athletics club used to work for me at the football club and I decided to make it my business to bump into him last week. After a few minutes of trivial talk, I began to get what I wanted from him. With a bit of prompting, I soon got him talking about the pills being offered to athletes at the club. To avoid suspicion, I made him think I was interested in the pills for my players. Told him I was looking for ways to increase their fitness levels for next season. Anyway, it wasn't long before he began to speak of the Stasi's grand plans for Olympic success. Muller almost spat out the next words from his mouth. "Anabolic steroids," he hissed. "Performance enhancing drugs. Those animals are giving those girls all kinds of pills to make them into the perfect running machines."

I sat there shell-shocked, trying to make some sort of sense of what Muller and his granddaughter were telling me.

"They've no idea what those drugs could be doing to those girls," Muller said, the anger burning through his cheeks. "Who can possibly know what damage is being done to their young bodies? How can these doctors fill these kids full of drugs and hope that there are no side-effects? I tell you Karl, I've ignored some pretty nasty things the Stasi have done over the years but this is something else. I can't tolerate this. I'll see out this season but I'm done with this club now. I don't recognise it anymore. I pulled Hanna out of the programme that very day and she won't ever go back. I can promise you that – no matter how much fuss the club kicks up."

I saw it now. It was clear to me why Muller had brought me here.

"You want me to warn Heidi don't you Mr Muller? You don't want her to be exposed to the same risks as Hanna."

"Karl – I am not a stupid man. I know that I can not make enemies of the Stasi lightly so I didn't explain the real reasons why Hanna left their athletics programme. It would not sit well with Erich Meier if he found out that I know about their doping experiments. I'd be putting myself and Hanna at risk. Of course, there is part of me that wants to blow the whistle on the whole thing straight away but something tells me it is not the right time. For now, I will have to be content with saving Hanna from further harm."

"And Heidi too," I said quietly.

"Yes," Muller nodded, "and Heidi too. I couldn't look you in the eye every day knowing what I do about the way the Stasi are developing their athletes."

"What about the other girls and boys?" I said. "Do you feel you could look their families in the eye if you were to bump into them?"

Muller sighed. "I could not – no – but there will come a time when I will speak out. Just not now. I can't put Hanna at risk and you must promise me that you will be discreet too. Speak to your sister of course. Do what you need to do but make sure this doesn't bring the Stasi to my door. As I've said, it is not wise to make an enemy of Erich Meier."

Chapter 22

I insisted Muller take me to my parent's house straight away. He argued that there wouldn't be time before the team left for France but I wouldn't listen. I had to speak to Heidi immediately. I couldn't just let things lie. As soon as the car pulled up outside the house, I leapt out and rapped impatiently on the door. My mother was out running some sort of errand but Heidi and my father were sat at the table having breakfast.

"Karl, what's wrong?" my father asked, alarmed. "I thought you would be on your way to France by now."

"I should be. Mr Muller's waiting outside now and I only have ten minutes at the most. I have to be quick."

I had so much to say but where could I start? How much should I say? Meier had already warned me about bringing my family into the Stasi's world. All of a sudden, I was lost for words.

"Karl – I hope this is important," Heidi said. "I thought you said you had to be quick. I've got to be at the club in twenty minutes and you're going to make me late the way you're going."

I stared back at her blankly. What was it that Erich Meier had mentioned about having someone take a hammer to her ankles? Would he really do that? Could he really be that evil?

"You can't go training today Heidi," I blurted out. "Not today, not tomorrow, not ever."

I could see the shock and confusion on their faces.

"Stop kidding about Karl," my father said. "Of course she will be training today. There is no reason why she shouldn't."

How much should I tell them? I thought to myself. How much can I say without putting them at risk?

"A friend of mine has told me that the coaches and doctors at Dynamo don't take care of their athletes properly," I said weakly. It's not the best place for you Heidi. You must leave as soon as possible."

My sister laughed at me and who could blame her? Even as the words left my mouth, I knew my argument was pathetic.

"You're talking nonsense Karl. I don't know what's got into you today," she said, a hint of irritation in her voice. Heidi had never been one to hide her feelings. "You concentrate on your beloved football and leave me to worry about my running. Either explain yourself or I have nothing more to say to you today."

"Dynamo don't care about you Heidi," I said. "They only see you as a way to make themselves look good. They don't care about you as a person."

"More nonsense Karl," she said, and now I could see the anger flashing in her eyes. "You have no idea how I am treated by the coaches. As a matter of fact, I'm very happy at Dynamo. This is all I've ever wanted Karl and it's not right that you should speak to me like this. No-one at the club has ever treated me badly so stop interfering or I will not forgive you."

I looked at my father helplessly but he wasn't about to offer me any assistance.

"Don't bring me into this Karl," he said.

I heard a blast from the car's horn outside. I couldn't stay much longer.

"Things will change Heidi," I said. "Things may be fine for now but they'll change. They'll make you take things that probably aren't right for your body. None of them actually know what harm they could be doing."

"What do you mean – take things?" she questioned.

I hesitated. I'd probably gone too far.

"Drugs Heidi," I said quietly. "My friend tells me that you will be given drugs to help improve your performance."

They were both stunned into silence for a moment.

"Karl, that's a bit strong," my father said. "How can you be sure? Who is this friend of yours who knows so much?"

"I can't say. I promised I wouldn't say."

"Then you shouldn't come here and talk like this," Heidi said, tears slowly trickling down her cheeks. I've never been given any drugs Karl – no one has ever mentioned anything like this to me. If they did, I'd refuse. I don't need any drugs to make me run fast."

I hated to see her upset like this. I took a step forward to embrace her but she stopped me in my tracks.

"No Karl – leave me alone. I hate you for this you know. You have no evidence of anyone doing anything wrong – just false, second hand gossip from some friend that you can't even talk about. I'm happy Karl – happy doing what I love. Can't you be happy for me too?"

I looked to my father again.

"I think she's right Karl," he said. "You have no evidence of this. Heidi is happy and that's what matters most. The minute that changes then I'll reassess things. Why don't you tell me who this friend is who speaks of all this?"

The car's horn blared out again. I can't tell you Dad, I thought to myself. I promised Muller and I have to keep to my word. You taught me that was important when I was a little boy. You're blind to what the Stasi are capable of though. Heidi too. They'll hook her in, just like they did with Hanna. Anyone who questions anything is punished. Who knows – the drugs may well be put into meals so that no one even notices they're taking them. Hanna told me she suspected as much.

"Do you know something Karl?" Heidi said sharply, as I stood in the doorway ready to go. "If Dynamo is such a terrible place to be, why haven't you left?"

I had no answer for her.

Chapter 23

The bus was already full when we boarded it. Muller and I had barely exchanged a word on the brief car journey to Dynamo's stadium, perhaps both still taking stock of the situations we found ourselves in. How on Earth was I going to prepare for a football match tomorrow evening? My head was a mess. Toni had saved a seat for me and I collapsed beside him.

"Somewhere more important to be Karl," he said, only half joking.

"I had a few things to sort out at home," I replied weakly.

He raised his eyebrows quizzically.

"Just family stuff Toni," I said. "Nothing to worry about. It'll soon blow over."

"Good – we need you to be at your best tomorrow Karl."

I nodded and leaned back into my seat.

"You would let me know if there's something bothering you wouldn't you Karl?"

"Yes – thanks Toni," I smiled.

Almost immediately, we set off, a coachload of about forty people altogether although only around half of them were players or club officials. The others, who sat towards the back of the coach, I'd never seen before in my life. I knew who they were though and why they were here. What I didn't know were the lengths they were prepared to go to in order to carry out their orders. Having had little to no sleep the previous night, I found my eyes growing heavy before I inevitably drifted off to sleep. I woke when I felt a hand shaking my shoulder. Groggily, I peered round my seat to see Emil's face. Damn it – Emil. In all the chaos and confusion that had unravelled today, I'd completely forgotten about him. He didn't say anything but simply gave me the slightest of nods. Tonight was the night.

No more than an hour later, we crossed the border into France and I felt a surge of exhilaration. Part of me wished that I could join Emil in escaping. Having been abroad on several occasions, my eyes had been well and truly opened to how East German propaganda portrayed life in the West and what the reality was. I was well accustomed to newspapers and state television advocating the success of East German society while seeking to depict the West in a negative light. Indeed, when I thought about it, sportsmen and sportswomen such as myself were symbols of East German strength and success. It was no wonder the Stasi sent so many men to watch us on trips across the border, as every defection was a clear signal that not everyone bought into the state's values.

So, after a long, tiring journey, we finally arrived at our hotel around nine o'clock local time. Apart from two security guards out front, it was extremely quiet and we were quickly paired off and allocated our rooms for the night. As planned, Emil and I made sure we were staying together. Carrying our holdalls to the elevators, we made our way to the third floor, which our party had been allocated for the visit. Of course, for every player, there was at least one unknown face preparing to watch our every move during the duration of our stay in France. On previous trips into Europe, I'd noticed that there would be at least two Stasi officers patrolling the corridors and ensuring that nothing untoward was occurring. Emil was utterly convinced that out rooms would be bugged and our conversations monitored so to finalise arrangements for his escape, we would have to seize an opportunity when the Stasi would not be watching. Straight after our arrival, before we'd all settled into our rooms, was the perfect time to catch them off guard.

As soon as we had dropped our bags off in our rooms, we were required to attend a brief team meeting in the hotel lobby and this was our chance. Just to the left of the elevators stood the men's toilets and, checking that no-one else was about, we both stepped inside.

"Half past eleven Karl," Emil said to me. "Do you know what to do?" I could see that he was agitated and who wouldn't have been in his position? It was a dangerous situation and I could feel my body trembling too.

"Yes," I nodded nervously. "I'll do it Emil. You can rely on me. Half past eleven. Be ready."

"Good. That's good Karl. Wish me luck alright."

"Yes – good luck Emil," I said quietly.

This wasn't the time for a long conversation. We needed to be at the team meeting promptly if we didn't want to arouse suspicion. Emil paused for a moment before holding out his hand.

"Thank you Karl. Thank you for everything."

With that, we walked through the door and back out into the corridor. Only after we'd walked half of the short distance to the lobby, did we hear the toilet door creak open behind us. When I turned, I saw Mr Muller's familiar large frame emerging. Ashenfaced, Emil looked at me, panic etched across his face. Had Muller been in one of the cubicles? He must have been. I cursed myself for being so stupid. Why hadn't we checked if we were alone. We'd been lucky – better it was Muller and not someone else. I could trust him – I was sure of it.

"Don't worry Emil," I whispered. "Even if the boss did hear us, he won't say anything. Trust me."

Emil stared right up me for a moment. Finally, he nodded and we made our way to the lobby.

Mercifully, the meeting was brief, lasting no longer than ten minutes or so. It made sense for the players to get a good night's rest before the big match tomorrow. When Emil and I returned to our room, I got myself ready for bed and lay down on top of the covers. Although I was tired, I had no intention of going to sleep.

Taking a look at my watch, I saw that it was now half past ten. Just an hour to go.Not knowing if the Stasi were listening in, Emil and I kept conversation to a bare minimum as we waited for the minutes to tick by. Thirty minutes, twenty, ten – lying there in the darkness worrying. I wondered if Emil felt as frightened as I did. I hoped he'd be OK. I hoped we'd both be OK. If things worked out the way we'd planned, Emil would be long gone by morning.

Half past eleven finally arrived. It was time. Clambering off my bed, I walked slowly to the door and opened it as quietly as possible. With the light from the corridor, I could just about see Emil's face staring back at me. He gave me a slight nod and smiled. I closed the door and as expected caught sight of the two men positioned at the end of hallway. If they were surprised to see me, they didn't immediately show it, remaining cold and impassive. The taller of the two of them seemed to question me with his eyes.

"I'm not feeling so good," I said, and to tell the truth, I didn't. The lack of sleep and anxiety I felt had left my skin cold and clammy while my stomach churned relentlessly.

"I just wanted to stretch my legs and get some fresh air," I continued. If I don't, I think I might be sick.

I studied their faces for any signs of a reaction, rubbing my hand across my temple and breathing out heavily in an attempt to convince them of my sickness. Finally, the tall man relented.

"There is fresh water in the lobby," he said. "You can get a drink from there. No more than five minutes though and it's too late to go outside. Be quick. I don't want to have to come looking for you."

I nodded my agreement and made my way to the stairs at the end of the corridor. My heart racing, I descended them as quickly as I could manage without drawing attention to myself. The second-floor passageway was empty but I carried on going, eventually stopping just outside the lobby on the ground floor. Making sure I didn't alert the member of staff who manned the reception desk, I tiptoed towards the dining room which stood a short distance away to my right. Unlike, the corridors, I was almost certain there would be no cameras here.

I didn't have long – a minute or so before the tall man began to look for me. Anxiously, I scanned the room for something I could use for the job in hand. Settling on a large ash tray sitting on top of one of the tables, I took a deep breath and struck the glass that protected the fire alarm positioned on the wall. The noise was excruciatingly loud, blaring out throughout the hotel. Emergency lighting flashed and a recorded fire drill message repeated over and over again.

A FIRE HAS BEEN REPORTED. PLEASE LEAVE YOUR ROOMS IMMEDIATELY. PROCEED TO THE MARKED FIRE EXITS. DO NOT USE THE ELEVATORS. THIS IS NOT A DRILL.

I had to move fast before anyone saw me beside the smashed glass. I slid out of the dining room and crouched down beside the flight of stairs that led to the first floor of the building. From above, I could hear the panic and confusion as feet tramped their way to the exits. Angry voices rang out in frustration as doors slammed open upstairs. The first wave of hotel guests were now making their way down the flight of stairs nearest to me, and as casually as I could, I slipped in with the crowd, following them outside into the hotel's carpark.

The next ten minutes were utter chaos as agitated guests stood in the cold outside as fire trucks arrived with their screaming sirens. I stood with the rest of the players to the far side of the car park, watching breathlessly as the fire crews entered the building. For this time of year, it was a cold night and I shivered. I could hear Toni complaining bitterly to Mr Muller, arguing that we were missing out on valuable rest. How would we be at our best for tomorrow's game after a long journey and an interrupted sleep?

"There's not even any smoke," I heard him say. "This is nonsense

Mr Muller. There's no fire in there. Someone's messing us about."

What he was expecting Muller to do I don't know. The fire crews had to do their job. Closer to the hotel, I caught sight of Erich Meier. He hadn't travelled on the coach with the rest of the squad, preferring to be driven to France by his personal chauffeur. Even from a fair distance away, I could tell he was furious. Deep in an animated conversation with two or three of his men, I watched as he called Mr Muller towards him. I had a fair idea what they would be discussing. Emil was nowhere to be seen.

Chapter 24

Finally, when the fire department had given us the all clear, we were free to return to our rooms. To be absolutely honest, I wasn't quite sure what to expect when I arrived at my door. Would Emil be inside with Stasi officers keeping him company? Would Meier be waiting there for me, knowing my involvement in Emil's escape? I remember feeling deeply unsettled as I turned the key in the lock. Just a short distance along the corridor, the tall man and his partner seemed to study my every move, their eyes boring into my back. Perhaps a little surprisingly, the room was completely empty. There was nothing to show Emil had ever been there. He and his belongings had disappeared. Trying to act casually, I had a quick wash in the bathroom before switching off the light and getting into bed. Alone with my thoughts, I kept waiting for the inevitable knock at the door. It never came and totally exhausted, I eventually managed a few hours of restless sleep.

At breakfast the next morning, no-one said a thing. It had always been drummed into us that it wasn't our place to ask unnecessary questions and with Erich Meier sitting at the head of the large dining table, this wasn't the place to start. Strangely, considering the events of the previous night, he seemed in good form this morning, laughing and mingling with the players. Finally, when everyone had finished eating, he stood and addressed the party.

"My boys," he said, "I stand here today a very proud man. This team has come a long way and I am confident that together we can achieve great things. Today could well be your greatest victory and I know you will not let me down. Good luck."

I sat there bemused. Our chairman was truly a man of many

faces. Without warning, he could switch from generous and jovial to cold and threatening.

"Finally," he continued, his face clouding over a little, "I must inform you that one of your colleagues has been sent home due to a breach of discipline. Of course, I know that you will respect that this is a private matter between him and the club. I trust it will remain that way."

It didn't take a genius to work out who he was talking about but no-one said anything. Once Meier had finished speaking it was like Emil had ceased to exist. No questions were asked and no further explanation given. It was like a dirty secret that you couldn't tell anyone about. For me, it was difficult to focus on the match against the French when my thoughts were elsewhere. Even as we warmed up before the game kicked off, I couldn't stop thinking of Emil. In my mind's eye, I could picture him sneaking away from the hotel as the fire alarm screeched out its warning, moving through the shadows on the way to his new life. However, almost immediately, images of his lifeless body, stretched out on the back seat of a white Sedan, flickered into my mind, blood oozing from a gaping bullet hole in his temple. It's fair to say that I was in no way prepared to play such a big game.

I've been told that the game itself was a bit of a thriller, ending 3-3 after a pulsating ninety minutes. Apparently, I performed well. For me though, it passed by in a blur, and to this day, I can barely remember anything about it. The only thing I fully recall is making sure I was seen to give my best, so afraid I was of Erich Meier noticing that I wasn't myself. Who knew what he'd do if he found out that it was me who'd set off the fire alarm. After the match, though, he certainly seemed in good spirits, entering the dressing room with a huge smile painted over his face and wrapping his long arms around the players. A draw away from home was a fantastic result for Dynamo, leaving us as favourites to win the tie with our home leg to come. If he knew it was me who'd helped Emil, he did a good job of hiding it.

"Brilliant performance Karl," he said embracing me warmly. "You've made me a proud man tonight. Thank you very much."

The following morning, I sat beside Toni at the breakfast table. He was almost buzzing with enthusiasm about our performance the previous night.

"Do you know Karl?" he said, "if we finish off the job next week, then it will be the greatest achievement in the club's history. We'll be part of that Karl – you and I. I always knew we could do it."

Toni still had so much passion for the game, talking about winning matches like an excitable schoolboy. For a moment, I wished I shared that joy he still experienced. It seemed so long ago since I'd felt like that, playing football like it was the only thing in the world that mattered, before my eyes were fully opened to what being part of Club Dynamo Berlin really meant. Before I'd learnt how the Stasi controlled East German football, before I realised that I belonged to them, before I'd learnt they planned to fill my sister full of drugs to help bring them glory. Before I was afraid. That's how I'd felt last night as I lay in my room alone, Emil's empty bed on the opposite side of the room.

"The semi-finals of the European Cup Karl," Toni continued. "That would be something to tell our grandkids about, would it not? We can win as much as we want in East Germany but to lift the European cup – well – that would truly be the greatest day of my life."

Despite myself, I couldn't help a small smile. Even with my hatred of Dynamo, the thought of winning Europe's biggest trophy was undeniably special. I forced this thought out of my head quickly.

"Do you think Emil is alright Toni?" I whispered quietly and watched his face darken immediately.

"I'm sure Emil is absolutely fine," he said, barely audible.

"Whatever rules he has fallen foul of is no business of ours anyway. It's between him and the club. Stay out of it Karl. It's not our concern."

"Emil's one of us Toni," I said. "It is our concern. We should care about him."

"Emil let the team down Karl. I've no idea why he was sent home early but he should have been out there playing last night. I'll tell him so when I see him next week."

If you see him next week Toni. *If* you see him. I thought to myself. With any luck, he'll be long gone by now.

Any further conversation was halted by Mr Muller who walked over to our table to inform us that the coach would be leaving in ten minutes. We were to collect our bags from our rooms and meet in the lobby promptly.

Within minutes, I'd collected up the few belongings that I'd brought with me and was packed up and ready to leave. Joining the rest of the squad in the lobby, I waited as the coach driver pulled up outside and began loading the bags into the baggage area beneath the vehicle. Stood beside Toni, waiting for our turn to get on board, I felt a hand on my shoulder. Instinctively, I turned around to face the tall man who'd stood guard outside my room for the last two nights.

"Mr Meier has requested that you and Toni accompany him in his personal car for the journey home," he said. "He'd like to talk some more about the match last night."

I was caught off guard. The last thing I wanted to do was to return home in Meier's car but how could I say no? Perhaps I shouldn't have been surprised. The chairman often liked a few of the players to accompany him on the return from an away match. As he often pointed out, he wanted to get to know the boys who played for him, enjoying listening to their thoughts about a game. I'd travelled back in his car before and he could talk enthusiastically for hours about football. I had to admit that he was engaging company too – larger than life, charming, with an opinion on just about everything. As long as you never crossed him, Meier could be like your favourite uncle. Even after threatening my family, he still greeted me with a warm smile and a handshake when he'd enter the changing rooms after a game. It was as if the chilling warnings that he'd issued me with had never left his lips. So, no, travelling back with Meier wasn't anything that should have set off alarm bells in my head but I felt uncomfortable all the same. Did Meier suspect that I had helped Emil escape? Would he ask me any awkward questions? Would he see the guilt in my eyes? I was grateful that Toni was getting in the car too. Somehow, this made me feel more secure.

As it happens, Meier seemed in excellent form as Toni and I sat in the back seat, the tall man taking the wheel in front.

"Karl, Toni, thank you for your company. I really appreciate it. It is a long journey home and Tomas here is not one for prolonged conversation," he said gesturing at the tall man. "He has no interest in this game of ours."

The tall man remained silent.

"You boys had me on the edge of my seat last night," Meier laughed. What a game you played. It is a good job I have no problems with my heart. What a performance. Now tell me boys, and I want your word on this, promise me that you will finish off the job in the home leg."

"Don't worry Mr Meier, we'll do our best," said Toni, a little apprehensively. I kept quiet. This was typical of the chairman. Full of warmth and encouragement when we had performed well. However, when Dynamo lost, and this wasn't very often, it would provoke a furious tirade after the match. It wasn't wise to make him promises that were difficult to fulfil.

"Do your best," Meier continued. "Come on Toni – I expect more confidence from a boy like you. I expect you to win. This will be the greatest achievement in Dynamo's history so don't you dare let me down."

He'd said this with a smile but I knew how desperate he was for this success, how it would hurt his pride if we were to be defeated on home turf, how angry he'd be.

We spent the next hour or so dissecting the previous night's match before finally the chairman grew tired of talking and we sat for the remainder of the journey in an awkward silence. Staring out of the window, I watched the trees glide by, their leaves a mixture of green and shadowy red. The last few days had taken their toll on my body and I felt my eyes begin to close before I drifted into a restless sleep filled with visions of Emil lying in a pool of his own blood and Heidi running away from me at full speed, refusing to listen to my cries for her to stop.

When I eventually awoke, we had made our way to the outskirts of Berlin. Toni's apartment was closer than mine and after giving the tall man the address, it wasn't long before we pulled up outside. A little wearily, Toni collected his bag from the boot, uttered a brief goodbye and entered the building. Away we rolled again and I began to look forward to getting home and resting my aching body. It was no more than a kilometre or so away. Perhaps only half-awake, I didn't recognise immediately that the tall man wasn't taking a direct route to my home. Initially, I thought that he might know a different route but it soon became clear that this wasn't the case.

"Excuse me Mr Meier," I said, "We're headed away from my apartment. We should turn around."

Without turning he answered me coldly. "Sit back Karl. We have somewhere else to go first. There's something you need to see."

What did he mean? Where were we heading? I felt my heart quickening.

"What is it I need to see Mr Meier?" I said, almost afraid of the answer. "Where are we going?"

"Please be quiet Karl," he said, looking straight ahead. "We will be there soon."

There was very little traffic on the road as we travelled across the city. Sitting in the back seat, I realised that even in some of the dark moments I'd been through in the last few years, I'd never felt this alone. I had no idea where the tall man was taking us but my instincts told me that I wasn't going to like it. It crossed my mind that I could possibly jump from the moving vehicle when it slowed down – perhaps make a run for it. I dismissed the idea quickly. Where would I run to? The Stasi had eyes everywhere in the city. Even if I escaped temporarily, I'd never be able to remain hidden. No, I'd have to remain calm and see how events unfolded. Outside, it was getting dark and a light drizzle was falling. Glancing through the window, I strained my eyes to see what was ahead. Then, emerging from the darkness, beyond the car's headlights, I saw it.

Chapter 25

•

Towering, grey concrete walls topped with barbed-wire loomed in front of our vehicle and I knew where we were. Officially, the place didn't exist and would not appear on any map but I had heard the rumours about the Hohenschönhausen. Here, the Stasi would hold anyone who had fallen foul of them. Everyone in East Berlin had heard horror stories of brutal interrogations and prisoners who had been held there for years without ever facing a fair trial. The car stopped briefly beside the huge, iron gates as armed guards, recognising Meier, quickly let us pass through into the complex. My throat felt as if it had been scraped with sandpaper. I sat in the back seat, trying to remain composed on the outside at least. Finally, we came to a halt and the tall man, got out and opened the car door on my right.

"Get out please Karl," he said calmly but firmly.

Somehow forcing my trembling legs to obey me, I did as I was told. What choice did I have?

"Walk with me Karl," Meier said as we entered the building, the tall man shadowing us a few metres behind. Through dimly-lit corridors we moved, as the fear igniting inside my chest grew and grew. Windows made from clouded glass provided what little light there was. On each side of me, were tiny, cramped cells, barely able to house any of the sorry looking inmates that lay on wooden bunks attached to the walls. Apart from a sink and a grimy looking toilet, they were empty. It occurred to me that I'd always thought that a prison would be a loud, disruptive environment, full of angry men furious to be imprisoned. Here though, it was silent. Most of the men had positioned themselves so that they would not face the opposite cells and there was no communication whatsoever. Somehow, this only added to the discomfort I felt.

Many of the prisoners were no older than me. Kitted out in ill-fitting blue tracksuits, they were a sorry sight, their skeletal like bodies showing the signs of a lack of good food. I found myself wondering what crime, if any, they'd been locked up for. It wasn't unusual for the Stasi to arrest anyone who opposed them politically. This could be anything from students distributing propaganda leaflets to citizens attempting to flee the country. Years of misery could await someone who had acted in a way they deemed a threat to the socialist government. No matter how hard I tried to hide my fear, I knew that it could soon be me in here. Locked up in solitude, not even a name anymore but a number.

I followed Meier through the block of cells and out into an empty courtyard. Crossing it briskly, we came to a set of stairs leading below the surface.

"Almost there Karl," Meier said as we descended. "Almost there."

My heart-beat quickening with every step, I took a deep breath as we came to a bleak underground environment, even more miserable than what I'd already witnessed. The cells here were even smaller than before. The single mattress that acted as a bed took up almost every inch of the space and the walls were covered in grime. In my head, I pictured myself lying there alone and afraid.

Whereas upstairs the blocks had mostly contained young males, there were now men and women of all ages. To my horror, in one cell, an old woman who must have been at least in her seventies lay back on a mattress. What on Earth she'd done to end up here I couldn't possibly imagine. It seemed the Stasi didn't discriminate when it came to age or gender. Nervously, my eyes scanned the length of the shadowy corridor. One room, if you can call it that, had so little space that it would only be possible to stand up at all times. After initially being puzzled as to why anyone would build such a small cell, I realised that this would be used as a punishment.

Anyone not complying with an interrogator would probably be left standing there until it was deemed that they deserved to be returned to a regular cell.

Meier caught me staring and stopped. He wanted me to see all this I thought. He wanted me to be afraid – to be intimidated, to see the desperate misery that could await me if I didn't do as he wanted. Another room was covered from floor to ceiling in black rubber cut from conveyor belts.

"To make the room hot and humid," Meier said without looking at me. "To encourage prisoners to talk openly to us if they want to live in greater comfort."

Striding forwards, Meier led the way to the very end of the corridor before stopping outside a cell in the far corner of the block. There was barely a glimmer of light here and I couldn't even be sure that there was anybody inside.

"Here we are at last Karl," Meier smiled. "I won't keep you long but there's something I felt you should see."

I hesitated for a moment, perhaps fearing what my eyes were about to witness. It was very dark inside the cell, and at first, I wasn't completely sure there was anyone in there. Straining my eyes, I looked inside, my head pounding furiously. I could just about make out the shape of the small bed and there did seem to be a figure lying on top of it.

"Go closer Karl," said Meier standing behind me, one of his large hands resting on my shoulder.

I leaned in so that my nose was pressed up against the bars. The was definitely someone lying there face down. I was so close to them that I could have reached my hand through the bars and touched the hair on the back of their head.

A low, guttural moan came from the body in the cell and to my horror, whoever it was reached out and gripped my arm! Terrified and in shock, my immediate response was to leap backwards and try to free myself but I quickly realised that the person in the cell wasn't trying to attack me but was desperate and disorientated. It was almost as if they were drowning and trying to reach out for safety. I stopped struggling and instead I clasped the hand in an effort to calm the person down. My eyes were growing accustomed to the dark now and as I looked down I could see a man's face.

"Emil," I gasped, "is that you?"

There was another groan from the darkness. It was him alright. His eyes were swollen and sore and his forehead was covered in large welts. A trickle of blood from a nasty cut snaked its way down his forehead and on closer inspection I saw that a tooth was missing from his mouth. What had they done to him? The savages – the absolute savages. My cheeks burning with rage and unable to control myself any longer, I span round quickly and lunged at Meier, at that moment intent on ripping him to pieces no matter what the consequences. Before I could reach him, the tall man sprang from the shadows and locked my arm behind my back. I struggled to break free of his iron grip but it only made him tighten it more.

"Don't be stupid Karl," Meier said calmly. "Let's not make things any more unpleasant. Remember that my man here is armed and a bullet to the kneecap would not do your football career any good. Stop struggling and walk with me."

I was in a no-win situation. Reluctantly, I did as he asked, sneaking a final, hopeless glance at Emil as we moved past his cell and back upstairs towards the courtyard. It wasn't long before we were back beside the car.

"Get in the back please Karl," the tall man said and I was not in any position to argue. This time he sat beside me in the back seat while Meier positioned himself behind the wheel. Before turning the key in the ignition, he turned around to face me."

"I know it was you who set that alarm off Karl," he said. "Remember that nothing remains hidden from me. Nothing."

I stared back blankly.

"You know Karl," he continued, you are my favourite player. I know I shouldn't have favourites but the way you play football is an example for any young boy wanting to wear the Dynamo shirt. It would break my heart if anything happened to you but I'm beginning to lose patience. Emil is a lucky boy you know. Any traitor of our country can consider themselves fortunate to be alive. He can rot in prison for the time being and think about how he's brought shame on the club."

I gazed out at the prison walls, trying to stop myself from shuddering.

"Do you know how easy it would have been to kill Emil?" Meier continued coldly. "How easy it would be to make it look like his car had come off the road in an unfortunate accident? Yes – Emil can count his blessings that I found it in my heart to forgive him despite the embarrassment he has caused me."

He fell silent for a moment, studying my face for a reaction.

"I'm not sure I could be so generous if you let me down again Karl. Like I said, it would truly break my heart. Remember that Karl."

In silence, we made our way to my apartment. I felt empty inside. Meier pulled up outside my front door but left the engine running.

"I expect you to make this up to me Karl, starting with the league match this week. I want to see you cover every blade of grass on the pitch – do you hear me? Every blade."

My head bowed, I nodded slightly.

Meier got out of the driver's side and opened the door beside me. A little cautiously, I climbed out and stood before him. To my surprise, he stepped forward into my personal space, gripping hold of my jacket and pushing his head towards my face.

"I'm hoping we can put this matter behind us now Karl," he said fiercely. "No more silly games. Do not cause me any more embarrassment please and don't even think of any attempts to leave the country yourself. Your life is here Karl, with me, with the club, for as long as I decide it is. Even if you managed to leave and another country takes you in, I can still find you Karl and then I will have a decision to make. Have no doubts though, that whatever I decide to do with you, your sister will be finished at Dynamo. Do you understand Karl? I am no monster and I will admit to you now that I would never carry out my threat to harm her in any way. But make no mistake, Heidi will never compete as an athlete again. She will never be a champion, never represent her country, never bring home a gold medal. If this happens Karl, it will be you who has crushed that girl's dreams and broken her heart. For this, she will despise you. You know that don't you Karl?"

I looked him right in the eye, not even trying to disguise my contempt. "Yes, Mr Meier. I know it would break her heart."

Chapter 26
Berlin 1970

I hear Muller's voice. "Karl, come on Karl. Let's get out there early – show the opposition that we mean business for the second half."

I'd been miles away, lost in my own thoughts.

"Sure," I tell him, just need to use the bathroom quickly first. This is a lie – I just need a minute to myself to get my head straight. I know what I have to do now. Today I'm going to leave East Germany for good. I've thought of nothing else this week and it's my only option. I know I'm going to have to be smart and find the right moment to slip away for I know that after Emil's failed attempt to reach the West and the part that I played in it, I will be being watched extremely closely. During trips abroad, the Stasi won't let me out of their sight and of course the border crossings are heavily guarded. But it can be done. Others have been successful in the past so why not me? It won't be easy – I know that and that's why now is the perfect time to slip away. At half-time during a big game. The only time of the week when the Stasi are not watching me – the only time I can catch them off guard. It almost gives me a strange feeling of pleasure to think of the confusion I'll cause when I fail to reappear for the second half. How long will it take them to catch on to my plans? Ten to fifteen minutes I'm guessing. Not long but long enough for me to disappear. I've got my car parked outside with spare clothes and enough food and money to get by for a while. I'm planning to lie low for a while and then pick a spot to sneak across the border.

I know what this will cost both me and my family and I hope

they can forgive me in time. I hope they understand my reasons. I run the tap and splash cold water on my face. I don't feel so good. Perhaps the strain of recent events has begun to show. Staring directly into the mirror, I can barely recognise my face. I am pale faced with haunted, tired eyes. It's difficult to believe that I am only twenty years old.

I turn, unlock the cubicle door and step back into the changing room. Grabbing my sports bag, I move out into the tunnel that leads out to the pitch but instead of turning right I will go to my left, back through the complex and the exit to the street outside. Before I have moved further than ten yards, a figure steps out from the shadows to confront me.

To my surprise, Muller has been waiting for me. He looks on edge, like something's on his mind.

"Somewhere you need to be Karl," he says as my heart sinks.

I've been caught red handed and I'm angry with myself. Angry that it is so obvious what I have been planning. Angry that I've been caught before even exiting the stadium.

"What the hell are you doing Karl?" he says with a hint of disappointment in his voice. How far do you think you will get? The Stasi must have close to a million people in this country who are working for them. Do you really think you can just drive off in your car and no-one will find you?"

I can't think of a single thing to say to him. Not one thing. Nothing.

"Even then," he continues, "we both know how difficult it is for anyone to cross the border, let alone someone whose picture will be sent to every crossing guard in the whole of East Germany. You will either end up getting shot or rotting away in prison for the next twenty years. Don't be a fool Karl."

I'm defeated. I don't know where to look and the stress of the last few weeks finally overwhelms me. I cover my face with my hands and I'm astonished when I feel Muller's arm around my shoulders.

"I need you to know that it wasn't me who gave Emil up to the Stasi," he says, "and I won't give you up either Karl. If you want to, you can walk out of here right now but I think you'd be making a mistake. This isn't the right time.

I'm caught off guard. I wasn't expecting him to come right out with it. In training, this week, he's kept his distance, not even mentioning anything about Emil. If he wanted to tell me he hadn't betrayed me, why now? I'd been convinced he'd been working for the Stasi all along – almost certain of it.

"I'm not sure what you mean Mr Muller," I say cautiously.

"Yes you do Karl. I heard you and Emil talking in France. I know what you had planned but I swear to you that I didn't say a word to anyone. Never have done. As I've told you before, I've turned a blind eye to the Stasi for as long as I can remember but I've never informed on anyone. In a month's time, I'll be finished here for good and I can promise you that I want to be able to look all my players in the eye and wish them well for the future."

"I don't know what to believe anymore. I'm tired of this – so tired," I tell him. "I want to trust you Mr Muller, I really do, but I don't think I trust anyone anymore. My family, Toni maybe, but no-one else."

Muller motions towards the pitch. "We don't have long Karl but this is the only place that I felt that no-one would be watching us. What can I do to make you trust me?"

I look right at him, studying his face for any tell-tale signs of dishonesty. The man has been like a second father to me but I just can't figure things out. He'd overheard me speaking to Emil that night. No-one else had been there and I hadn't told a soul. It had to have come from him. There was no other possibility. Then it strikes me, an awful thought so terrible that I try to dismiss it immediately but the more I think about it, the more it makes sense. I feel my eyes welling up.

"I want you to help me cross the border Mr Muller," I say suddenly. "I know it's a lot to ask but I'm begging you."

The words just seem to escape from my mouth without me having full control over them. As soon as they slip out, I know that I am taking a risk. If Muller is indeed a Stasi informant, I am leaving myself completely exposed and who knows what Erich Meier will do with me. For all I know, I could be in a cell next to Emil before the day is over.

Muller seems taken aback too and who can blame him? It isn't the sort of favour you get asked every day.

"Please Mr Muller," I continue. The only way I can get my sister out of Dynamo for good is if I defect. My family name will be dirt and there's no way Meier will let her compete as an athlete in this country again. He's told me as much himself. What he doesn't realise is that's exactly what I want. Please Mr Muller. Heidi won't listen to me. She's too headstrong – too focused on achieving her dreams to worry about what it might cost her. Please help me save her from destroying herself."

Muller watches me closely for a moment. His face gives nothing away. Whatever he's thinking, it is impossible for me to tell. Finally, he responds.

"We'll talk later Karl," he tells me, turns and walks out onto the pitch.

Chapter 27

Having thrown my bag back into the changing rooms, I follow Muller back onto the pitch, barely making it out in time for the kick-off. Toni's furious with me and doesn't make any attempt to hide it. My head's not on the game and he knows it.

"Come on Karl," he barks at me from the centre circle. "Get a hold of yourself. I need more from you."

I ignore him and take up a position on the left flank. The game kicks off and I'm all over the place. My touch is awful and all the energy seems to have been drained from my body. I'm no use to the team whatsoever but our one and only substitution has already been used due to an injury to our left back in the first half.

Our opponents have several chances to equalise but luck, along with the referee, is not on their side and around the hour mark, one of our centre backs thumps in a header from one of Toni's accurate corners. My team-mates surround him, offering him their congratulations but, having been left back on the half way line to defend against a counter attack, I trudge wearily towards the dugouts to take a drink of water. My head is still throbbing with pain and I need to take a minute to rest. Before I reach the touchline however, I am intercepted by Mr Muller. He wraps an arm round me and begins whispering into my ear. To anyone watching from the stands, this seems completely innocent – just a manager offering his player instructions but this is nothing of the sort.

"Five more minutes Karl," Muller tells me, "then go down and feign an injury. After I take you off, wait for me in the changing rooms."

I look back at him, a little perplexed.

"Pensioners are allowed a pass to cross the border Karl," he says. "My car is outside."

This is no time for prolonged conversation but immediately I understand. For the last five years or so Berlin's elder generation have been allowed to cross the border and travel to the West. This could be for a period of up to four weeks and citizens are permitted to visit relatives once a year if they have filled in the appropriate paperwork to secure a travel permit. Basically, the authorities are not concerned at the prospect of elderly East Berliners defecting as the economy has little need for them. In fact, I don't know of anyone who hasn't returned home and it is usually seen as an opportunity for people to bring back Western goods for their families. Like most people in the city, I know Muller has relatives who live in the West and he takes up the opportunity to visit them when it is presented. I've heard that he is quite fond of bringing back a bottle or two of French wine but this time it won't be alcohol that will be hidden away in his car – it will be me. Goodness knows how he plans to do it but that can wait for now. One thing at a time.

All of a sudden, I'm exhilarated. The adrenaline surges through my veins and I feel I can run through brick walls, when just minutes earlier, it seemed like every step I took, I was walking in thick treacle. I run as hard as I have done all season to try and control the restless energy that consumes my body. Five minutes, I think to myself, probably the last five minutes I'll spend on a football pitch. I picture myself hiding under a pile of blankets in the back of Muller's car and it's frightening and exciting in equal measures. I could either be starting a new life this evening or lying in a morgue. I'm grateful to Muller too, and sorry that I've ever doubted him. In this country, it's so difficult to fully trust anyone, so hard not to become paranoid, so hard to see things with a clear mind. I worry about him too. He's risking everything to help me. I hope I can persuade him to stay with me in the West but I know that he has his daughter and granddaughter here in Berlin. I don't think he'll be able to leave them behind.

In saying that, I didn't think I'd ever leave my family behind either but the way I figure it, I have no choice. I know I'll be saving Heidi from becoming part of some vile experiment. I can't just stand by and watch my sister being used like that. She's too innocent to realise that she's just a pawn in a corrupt system and too stubborn to listen to people like me who try to tell her the truth. I guess when you believe in something so passionately, as my sister does with her running, you're blinkered to anything negative about it. I'm not angry with her – just frustrated. My parents on the other hand. I love them very much but if I'm honest about it, I'm angry with them. They think I've grown bitter and paranoid about Dynamo and that I'm foolish for believing every bit of dressing room gossip I hear. Well, maybe I have grown paranoid but with good reason. I've seen the evil face of the Stasi and I know exactly what they are capable of. When all is said and done though, it's going to break my heart to do this to them and I just hope that one day they'll forgive me.

Despite my furious running, I'm still very much on the periphery of the game. The ball just doesn't seem to drop my way. The five minutes Muller asked me to wait are rapidly elapsing and I begin to think of how I will feign injury. Of course, I've never done anything like this before. How should I go about it? Some sort of muscle pull would probably be the best option and I try and run through what I will do in my mind. While I do so, we win a corner and I take up my usual position on the edge of the penalty area. Toni hits one of his vicious, in-swinging crosses and I watch as the ball cannons off a defender's knee and bounces up towards me. The spin on the ball makes it difficult to strike on the volley but I catch it cleanly and it flies towards goal, just as the opposition's centre back clatters into me with a desperate, last-ditch lunge. Of course, I have no interest in helping Dynamo win the match but I cannot deny the thrill I feel as the ball strikes the net and the crowd erupts. It's an involuntary action I suppose and if these are to be my last minutes on a football pitch, then I'm pleased that I can finish with a special goal like this. Then the pain hits me. The full weight of the centre back's heavy frame has landed on my ankle and immediately I know I'm in trouble as I've had this type of injury before. Twisted ligaments – nothing too serious but enough to leave me hobbling about for the next two or three weeks. I remember how my whole foot swelled up like a balloon the last time it happened and how I used to sit at home with a frozen packet of peas over it. A sudden panic washes over me. Will I still be able to make my escape? The ankle's painful and not ideal but I should still be able to put some weight on it. At least I don't actually have to feign injury anymore. I wonder if Muller thinks I'm genuinely hurt or if I'm faking. He probably thinks I'm an incredible actor.

Although it's unlikely I'll need it, Muller sends the stretcher team on, trying to make things more convincing. The physio's lift me onto it and I'm heading towards the dressing room as planned. We've almost reached the touchline when I feel a hand grip mine. It's Toni.

"Great finish Karl," he tells me, "I knew you could give more and you didn't let me down. Let's hope the injury is not too bad. Catch up with you later Karl."

He goes to pull his hand away but I clasp it tightly, gripping it so hard that I can feel him wince with pain. I'm angry – angrier than I've ever been with anyone in my whole life yet at the same time I feel remarkably clear headed.

"You were my best friend Toni," I tell him. "Like a brother to me and I'd have done anything for you." I tightened my grip further, digging my fingers into the palm of his hand and looking up into his reddened face. "I know it was you," I say and finally let go. I don't look back.

I ask the physios to sit me down in the changing rooms and give me an ice pack for the ankle. I tell them it's not too bad and ask them to give me a bit of space. Thankfully, they do just that and I'm left on my own. I realise that my whole body is shaking and I sit back against the wall and cover my face with my hands. Through the gaps between my fingers, I see the clock on the dressing room wall reading quarter past four and there is approximately half an hour until the game finishes. We don't have much time but all I can do is wait.

I wonder how long Toni has been feeding information on me to the Stasi. Was it from the moment we broke into Dynamo's first team? I remember how young I was when they first tried to dig their claws into me and how difficult it was to resist. I remember how frightened I'd been when Erich Meier had asked me to inform on my team-mates. I'd just wanted to play football and he'd threatened to take that away from me. It would have been so easy to give into his demands. I could picture Meier having the same conversation with Toni – telling him that he was finished at Dynamo unless he did as he was told. With his ambition, Toni would never have been able to contemplate a life without football. I can imagine him agonising over his decision and for a moment I pity him. Despite what he's done, Toni's not a bad person. I still believe he cares about me and considers me a friend, but he's managed to dig himself into a dark hole that he can never truly escape from. He almost certainly isn't the only player in the team on the Stasi's payroll – not that it would have been about the financial rewards for him. Meier will have known exactly what to say to him. He will have understood Toni's character, seen that burning determination to be a winner and used it to his own advantage. To begin with it will more than likely have been little things that Meier asked for – just a few snippets of information that had no real consequences for anyone involved. This will have progressed gradually, giving Toni the impression that what he was doing wasn't such a big deal, until the Stasi had him completely under their control. Then there would have been no way back. So, right now, I'm angry with Toni but in time I think it will be more of a deep sadness that I will feel.

My thoughts are interrupted by the door swinging open. Muller walks into the changing room.

"You ready?" he asks me, "I've told the others that I've gone to check on you so we have a little time but not much."

"I'm good," I say, rising a little unsteadily to my feet before hobbling towards the door.

"You weren't faking," he says, surprised. It looks bad Karl. Are you alright to walk?"

"I'll be fine," I tell him, although the pain increases with each tentative step I take.

Cautiously, the two of us walk out into the tunnel area before turning left into the main corridor that leads out to the reception desks. Walking proves to be difficult for me and I have to lean on Muller for support. It strikes me that we look like an extremely odd couple shuffling along.

We pass the reception desks that are manned by just one elderly lady who has worked there for as long as I can remember. Muller, who has always made it his business to get to know every member of staff, gives her a smile which she returns warmly.

"This boy needs to have an x-ray on his ankle," he says to her. "I am going to drive him there myself. If anyone asks, can you please tell them where I can be found?"

The woman nods politely and we move outdoors into the car-park. Thankfully, Muller's blue Trabant is only a short distance away and I am able to clamber in and take my place in the passenger's seat. As I do so, we hear a roar from the crowd. For a split second, it makes me anxious but I realise that it is too early for the final whistle. There must be at least quarter of an hour remaining. Dynamo must have scored again.

Muller turns the key in the ignition and we're away, heading across the city and towards the border checkpoint. He drives steadily; there is no point in attracting unwanted attention.

"Are you sure about this Mr Muller?" I ask. "I know what he's risking to help me."

"I'm sure Karl," he replies, his gaze on the road ahead.

I keep quiet for a while but I can't stop thinking of what the Stasi will do to him. All of a sudden, my mind is clouded by self-doubt. I'm prepared to risk my own life to escape but now that someone else is involved I'm apprehensive.

"But Mr Muller," I begin, the Stasi will...

"Karl," he interrupts, "I am an old man now. I have very little of my life to live. It's not as if I am going to spend the next twenty years in prison. Now, keep quiet. You need to be focused."

To my surprise, Muller turns into a tight alleyway and stops the car. There is nobody about.

"Don't get out Karl," he tells me, before getting out and walking round to the front of the car. He opens the bonnet and I hear him fumbling about. Feeling the knot that has formed in my stomach tightening, I can't help cursing Muller under my breath as the time ticks by. There is no time for this. Finally, he finishes whatever it is he is doing and I feel a light rap on my window. I open the door and make a clumsy attempt to rise to my feet. By now, my ankle is throbbing angrily and I lean into Muller for support.

He helps me hobble to the front of the car and there I see it. Muller's vehicle has been modified so that there is a space between the engine block and the interior. At first glance, it seems inconceivable that a grown adult could squeeze inside it and I stare at Muller quizzically.

"I like to bring the family a few things back from my trips to the West," he tells me. "The checkpoint guards don't suspect a thing."

"But you can't possibly expect me to fit in there," I say, unable to take my eyes off the cramped compartment.

"I don't expect it to be comfortable for you Karl. I imagine it will be excruciating but there is no other way I can smuggle you across the border. It is an hour or so of your life Karl. A hellish hour no doubt but just an hour. Then you can leave East Germany behind for good. Now come on, we don't have a great deal of time."

I wince with pain as Muller lifts me up and pushes me feet first into the empty space. There is so little room that I can't fully extend my legs and I have to push against the far side of the car and lift my knees a little. This doesn't do much for my ankle and I have to stifle a scream of pain by biting down on my lip. Eventually, I manage to manoeuvre my body so that I can just about fit inside although every muscle I have now seems to ache.

"One hour Karl," Muller reminds me. "One hour."

He reaches into the back seat of the car and returns with a blanket.

"You need to pull this over the top of you," he tells me. "They will be using thermal cameras. This should be thick enough to retain the heat that your body generates."

I nod, barely able to believe I am agreeing to such madness and Muller tucks the blanket over me. I can see nothing but blackness now.

I feel the car begin to roll forward. I close my eyes and try to relax my body but it is impossible to find any sort of comfort. The heat from the engine is stifling and I can feel the perspiration forming on my forehead before trickling slowly down my face. My eyes feel heavy and sore and with every bump in the road that Muller hits, I groan in pain. It is difficult to breathe and I have to force myself to defy the rising sense of panic I feel. One hellish hour I remind myself – just one more hellish hour.

As I lie there with my lungs screaming for fresh air, I feel a sudden overwhelming sorrow. I might never see my family again and I'm not sure they'd want to anything to do with me anyway. After defecting, I'll be painted as a traitor. All manner of lies will be spread about me in order for the country to save face and I imagine that life will be pretty uncomfortable for my parents for a while. Then there's Heidi of course, and when I picture her face when she's inevitably thrown out of the athletics programme, it makes me feel terrible. I hope that in time she will understand that this was the right thing for me to do. I hope in time she will forgive me. I was happy here once. Even with the political turmoil that surrounded the building of the wall, I enjoyed my childhood. Of course, our family never had much but then who did? It never bothered me one bit – not even for a minute. I had my football and I had my friendship with Toni. It was all I needed. I have neither now. I'm going to force myself to remember the good things about Toni – before the Stasi got their hooks into him. I'll try and think of the hours we spent at the playground, kicking his old ball against the concrete wall with a small goal painted onto it. I'll remind myself of his sense of humour and how he'd lift my spirits when I'd had a bad game. I don't want to hate him.

It's not a long drive to the checkpoint and we must be getting close now. The car slows to a halt and I realise that we are in a queue. I can hear the soft rumbling of other cars' engines. Gradually, we inch our way forwards until eventually I can hear the border guards' voices. It's difficult to tell exactly but I'm certain we can be no more than twenty meters from passing through the checkpoint. I hear a guard asking a woman to get out of her vehicle so she and her car can be searched. When travelling abroad with the team, I've seen this sort of thing before – the intimidation, the suspicion, some people being led away at gun-point, others left alone. There never seems any sort of logic to who is stopped and who is allowed to cross the border without any hassle. I've seen guards x-ray the most trivial of objects such as hairbrushes and shoes before.

We creep slowly forwards once more and I hear Muller wind his window down and a guard's footsteps getting closer and closer. He pats the front of the car with his hand as he approaches and I feel myself holding my breath and hoping that he will not hear my drumming heart pumping furiously away. Perhaps it's the tension, but my legs are cramping unbearably and it takes all my strength to keep completely still and quiet. My throat feels like it has been scratched with sandpaper as I try and run through in my mind what I will say if I am discovered. There's not much I could really do to explain myself I suppose. If the guards don't shoot me on the spot, then I can expect to be in Meier's prison for the rest of my days.

"I will need to see your papers," I hear the guard say to Muller, and I listen as he fumbles about before handing them over. Then there is a long silence. An agonising wait, as I picture the guard finding something to his dissatisfaction and having the car taken apart from top to bottom. Keep calm, I tell myself silently. Keep calm and this will be over soon. There's no reason for the guards to have any suspicions. This isn't the first time that Muller's crossed the border.

"Is there a problem?" I hear Muller ask.

Still silence. What is the guard waiting for? I listen to his footsteps as he walks to the rear of the vehicle and opens the boot. He rummages around roughly for a while, perhaps searching for some sort of hidden compartment. The force of his movements cause the car's chassis to shake and I worry that he will hear my body bumping against the panels that I am pressed up against. I'm helpless. All I can do is wait.

"I need you to step out of the car," the guard tells Muller and I feel my stomach lurch. The door swings open with a creak and Muller gets out.

"I will have to look in your bag and check your papers," the guard tells Muller and I presume he has complied as I can soon hear him rustling about inside Muller's holdall. This seems to take an eternity and does nothing for my stress levels.

"Your name is Muller," the guard says. "I know your face from somewhere don't I?"

My heart begins to pound its furious beat once more, sending my blood surging through my veins. Where is this leading? Does this guard know that it is the manager of Dynamo Berlin attempting to cross the border? Will it matter?

"The football club," Muller replies without hesitation. Club Dynamo."

A short silence follows. I can almost hear tiny cogs in the guard's mind whirring away.

"Don't Dynamo have a match today?" he asks.

"Finished a couple of hours ago," Muller replies, unflustered. "I wanted to make a quick getaway – family to visit, that sort of thing. The sooner I can get that out of the way, the sooner I can return. As I'm sure you know, we have a big match to play in midweek and I need to be back in good time – have to keep my players on their toes."

Another uncomfortable wait. I can neither see nor hear anything now. Finally, I hear Muller get back into the car and start the engine. This is it I think and grit my teeth. This is actually going to work. Muller's going to pull it off. The exhilaration I feel takes my mind off the pain that my entire body is gripped by. We begin to roll forward and then I hear the guard shout.

"Stop there," he shouts suddenly and I feel my heart drop through my chest.

"I forgot to ask," the guards says to Muller. "What was the score? Did you win?

"By three goals," Muller responds. How he stays so calm I do not know.

"That's good," the guard replies. "Have a safe journey Mr Muller."

I feel the car move on through the checkpoint. Five seconds, ten seconds, twenty – are we through I wonder? We drive for a period of a minute or so before stopping briefly, then we are away again, this time moving more quickly. My mind is moving at one hundred miles per hour. We must be across the border by now surely. Why hasn't Muller pulled over? Is anyone following us? Just when I think that my aching body can endure no more, the vehicle stops. I listen as Muller exits the driver's door and pulls the catch to release me from my temporary prison. I see his rugged face looking down at me and he smiles, helping me, with some difficulty, to free myself from the confined space I have lain in for the last hour and a half. I try and stand but my wounded ankle betrays me and before Muller can prevent me from falling, I collapse in a heap on the ground. It is still wet from the afternoon's rain and the damp seeps into my clothes as I lie at the side of the road. For now, I don't care though. I've reached the West and my second life has just begun.

Chapter 28
East Berlin - 1995

So much time has passed since I started my second life in 1970. It has taken me twenty-five years to return to East Berlin and confront my past. On the table in front of me are files that the Stasi kept on me during my time at Dynamo Berlin. Although they've been available to me for some time, I just haven't been ready to face them until now. There are too many ghosts buried in my past and if I'm honest, I've been afraid to confront them. My time at Dynamo Berlin still weighs heavily on me after all these years.

I hold the thick folder in my hands for a full minute before I open it. Not that it can ever ease the trauma I went through. I want to understand what happened and somehow bring some closure on that period of my life. It's been five years now since the Berlin wall was torn down. I remember that night in November, watching the television footage of the thousands of East Germans flooding towards the border crossings, demanding to leave the country immediately. I never thought I'd live to see that moment and even from the other side of the world, it stirred up feelings inside me that had long remained dormant. That night, I thought of the family I'd left behind in 1970. The family from my first life. I thought of my father, who I'd barely communicated with in twenty years and Heidi who now had two little boys of her own – my nephews that I'd never met.

You see, as I'd feared, Erich Meier didn't take kindly to me defecting to the West. It was a huge embarrassment to him and I'd always known that he'd try and take his revenge. The news that I'd fled the country sent out a very negative signal, and at first, I understand that there wasn't much in the newspapers at all. Then came the smear campaign, with the inference being of course, that I was influenced only by money and had been offered it in large amounts. Seduced by capitalists was pretty much the gist of it. Muller got pretty rough treatment too. Not only was he accused of having taken a financial reward for helping me escape but he was also painted as an old man with an alcohol problem. There were some vicious lies circling about him in East Berlin that caused a great deal of pain to his family. In fact, Muller took some convincing not to return home. He had his daughter and granddaughter of course and found it hard to come to terms with the fact that he could no longer see them. It was a difficult situation but a return to East Germany would have meant a prolonged spell in prison at best. Muller's family wouldn't have wanted that but it didn't stop the sharp pangs of guilt that I felt. The man had given up his family for me.

As for my family, as there was no way they would be allowed to receive an incoming call from the West, I tried writing to them to explain my actions. However, there was a problem. I knew that any post that they received would have been intercepted by the Stasi first. Even if my letters did reach my loved ones, then I had to be careful about what information I decided to include. I couldn't tell them that I'd wanted to blacken my family name to have my sister thrown out of Dynamo's athletics programme. Erich Meier could never learn of my intentions. Therefore, I kept things quite mundane, apologising for leaving them and promising that I'd be in touch soon.

The first reply I received was written by my father, and sure enough, I ended up getting what I wanted. Heidi was dismissed from Dynamo as a direct result of my defection but the Stasi didn't stop there and the threats and intimidation began almost immediately. Firstly, another family was moved into my parent's house without any explanation or negotiation and it was clear that life would be made as difficult as possible for them. In my father's letter, he also talked of a delegation from Dynamo that were prepared to give me an opportunity to change my mind. If I realised my big mistake and made a full apology, then they would still welcome me back with open arms. My sister would be reintroduced to the athletics team and the housing situation would be re-assessed. My father let it be known quite clearly how I'd broken Heidi's heart – broken all of their hearts. Apparently, my sister could barely get out of bed in the mornings because of the pain I'd caused her. It was extremely difficult not to give in and return with my head bowed. Deep down though, I knew this was a trap. Defecting was an act of treason – a criminal act, and there was no way I would be forgiven so easily. I would be made an example of. That much I was certain of. Another thing that bothered me was the nagging thought that my father's words had been doctored. Much of the letter rang true but some parts didn't seem like his voice speaking to me. You see, my father was not by nature an overly emotional person and yet his letter was often the exact opposite. I couldn't be sure but I was aware that the Stasi would more than likely have seen what had been written. Would they have changed parts of it to suit their needs?

Adjusting to a new life was difficult but I had made my decision and now I had to get on with living. I was granted asylum in West Germany and having taken my time to get my head straight, I took up the offer of a trial with Hamburg, one of the Bundesliga giants. Initially, I was a bit off the pace which considering what I'd been through, was hardly surprising. I also had my doubts about whether I should ever set foot on a football pitch again. Having fallen out of the love with the game, I wondered if I had the heart for it anymore. I didn't want to cheat Hamburg and their fans either; I had to give them my best effort or walk away. In the end, Muller, who had taken on a scouting role at Hamburg, convinced me to give it another go. As he said, I was still a young man, with my best footballing years ahead of me. Besides, I needed to earn a living somehow.

To my surprise, I actually began to enjoy football again and the atmosphere at Hamburg was completely different from anything I'd ever experienced at Dynamo. Players enjoyed a laugh and a joke and I didn't spend my time looking over my shoulder, paranoid that one of my team-mates was watching my every move, listening to every conversation. As a first team appearance for Hamburg drew nearer, I felt like I could make the most of this second opportunity. However, it proved difficult to make a clean break from the clutches of the Stasi.

The next letter was from my mother and took things a step further. She informed me that my father had lost his job and that they were struggling to put food on the table. Wherever my parents went, they felt a deep sense of shame, almost as if they were thieves and had stolen something. No-one wanted anything to do with them anymore and didn't want to risk any association with a family that had raised a criminal. Again, she went on to talk about meeting with Dynamo and the opportunity for me to be reintegrated into the team. All would be forgiven and I would have a clean slate. Although I suspected this letter had been doctored too, it was deeply upsetting all the same.

Living in West Germany was different to say the least. One thing that I noticed in particular was the complete lack of politics. Back in East Berlin, you could never escape it. Whether you flicked on the radio or bought a newspaper it was always socialism. Every billboard promoted it, there were flags everywhere and pictures of Karl Marx in every window. From the day that I was born, I realised that I'd been told how to behave, how to think and what to believe. I was very conscious that I was different to the other players at Hamburg and that it wasn't easy fitting in. It was as if I'd arrived in a completely new world where nothing was as I expected it to be. I actually remember being completely astounded when I saw some of the other players throwing food away after eating in the canteen. I'd never seen anyone waste food before.

Still the letters from home continued to arrive, each one more bitter in tone than the last. My paranoia continued to grow. I knew that to some extent my family would be angry with me but did they really hate me? One letter from my mother even informed me that she had contemplated suicide and I became so racked with guilt that it was difficult to function. I kept telling myself that this couldn't be true but how much did I really know? I wrote back every week and tried to tell my parents how much I loved and cared about them but I became more and more convinced that my letters were never received, at least not how they were originally written. It dawned on me that in starting my new life I'd lost everyone that I'd loved from my old one.

Chapter 29

Finally, I plucked up the courage to open the files and started to read. Once I've begun, I can't stop. It's all there and just as awful as I've always suspected – the plotting, the betrayals, the constant surveillance. It seems like half of East Berlin has been collecting information about me at some point, including neighbours, a girl I'd known since primary school and of course my best friend Toni. The ugly details were there in black and white. Flicking through pages and pages of reports, I find the time when he was first recruited.

Area Command
Department VIII
Surveillance of Karl Littman
Re: Recruitment of teammate and friend Toni Schneider
Meeting duration – 1 hour and 15 minutes.

At around 2:30pm on 23.11.67, the subject named above was brought into the People's Police Station with the purpose of enlisting him as an informant. The meeting began with Schneider being asked to confirm the details of his background which he did without any unnecessary fuss. With regards to his sporting career, he was in agreement with us that his life had reached a crossroads. He could either provide information to the People's Police or his position at Sporting Club Dynamo could no longer be guaranteed. The subject seemed agitated at first and took longer than expected to break. Pleasingly, because at one stage this wasn't a certainty, it can be reported that he ended up being in safe hands, having finally agreed to the conditions set before him. Once he had signed the relevant papers, he was assigned his first mission, which was to report back to us the conversations of player X and player Y who are currently being monitored with regards to their political views.

Even after all these years, it hurts me deeply to think of the moment I lost my best friend to the Stasi. I feel a lump in my throat but my eyes remain drawn to the page. I can see the very document that Toni put his name to and began his betrayal.

I Toni Schneider *am prepared to support the Ministry for State Security in carrying out its operations. I commit myself to report without delay, any matters, rumours or indications of any crimes, that could lead to damage to the democratic process of our country. Furthermore, I commit myself to justify the trust placed in me by maintaining unconditional silence about my connection to any officers of the state. I am aware that breaking this code of silence will aid enemies of this country and will result in prosecution and the removal of my freedom. For reasons of vigilance, I will submit my reports under the Alias of 'Ursel'. I will attend my agreed meetings with my representatives regularly and will carry out missions to the very best of my ability.*

"Oh Toni," I think to myself. "You just couldn't let them take your football away could you? You couldn't bear the thought of working away each day in a normal job without the thrill of scoring a goal or winning a match to look forward to and once they'd got their hooks into you, there was never going to be any way out."

I keep reading and feel the tears forming in my eyes as I find the first report he submitted about me.

1.9.1968 – Report submitted by Ursel
Subject: Littman Karl
I have known Karl Littman for many years now and I have noticed a change in his behaviour recently. Whereas once he was content

at Sporting Dynamo, recently he has shown a dissatisfaction with the team and has begun to ask questions with regards to the club's integrity. During the last few weeks, he has made noises about leaving the team behind altogether and I believe he means it. Although this situation will require monitoring, Karl is a quiet, shy person and there is no need to fear that he will share his thoughts with many people. He only spends time with a few close friends and his immediate family. I believe that he is of good character and with the influence of the club, can still be a great asset to the team. I am certain that he has no contacts in the West and in moral terms, I hold him in high esteem.

"I'm glad you held me in high esteem Toni," I think to myself. "If only you had shown more of these morals that you talk about. You talk about me in such glowing terms and yet you were prepared to spy on me for the Stasi. You couldn't live with the guilt either could you? Look at you now. Once that knee injury finished your football career prematurely, you had nothing left."

1.9.1968 – Report submitted by Ursel
Subject: Littman Karl

My recent surveillance of Karl causes me a little concern. I fear that he has become heavily influenced by Emil Lang, one of his more senior team-mates, and that defection is not out of the question. I am not sure if any such action is imminent but I believe the situation should not be taken lightly. I must stress that I am of the opinion that Emil is the one who talks of moving to the West and that as far as I understand it, Karl has no intention of dishonouring his family by carrying out such a foolish act. However, he is a loyal character and it would not surprise me if he were to attempt to assist Emil with his plans. It would be wise to pay close attention to them while I gather further information.

There it is. Conformation of what I'd always believed and why I can't ever forgive Toni. I don't hate him but neither can I bring myself to make contact and talk things through. I do feel sorry for him though and I understand that life has been difficult for him after his football career ended. He never married or had children and from what I've been told, he spends most of his time inside the house he shares with his father. It strikes me as rather sad that someone once so energetic and full of life can barely bring himself to move from his armchair.

There is just one more thing I have to know before I leave these files behind forever and continue with my second life. It was the day before my debut for Hamburg when I decided that I was giving up football for good and leaving Germany. I'd talked to Muller about my fears that the Stasi could still target us now we were in the West. I knew the humiliation that we'd caused Erich Meier and that he'd stop at nothing to ensure we were punished somehow. Although Muller told me I was probably imagining it, I became convinced that there were Stasi operatives watching me, following my every more, plotting to kidnap me and bring me back to East Germany. I'd wake in the night, covered in streams of sweat, and scream at non-existent intruders. Then, the next morning, I'd be irritable and exhausted. Not surprisingly, this had a negative effect on my performance at training.

I began to realise that I'd never truly leave the Stasi behind unless I left Germany altogether. I was upfront about my intentions to Hamburg, and although they tried to change my mind, they respected and understood my decision. In fact, they went out of their way to support me. One of their ex-players was the manager of the New York Cosmos team in the United States of America and although I was adamant I was finished with playing football, he had something that the club thought would interest me. The Cosmos hired a certain number of staff that would be responsible for promoting sport for school children in the community – a sort of club ambassador to set up clubs and opportunities to get young people active. It was perfect for me and I jumped at the chance to go and live and work in the States. I was to leave in less than a week and I felt like a weight had been lifted off my mind. There was just one more thing I had to do before leaving.

I found it hard to tell Muller that I was leaving. Ever since arriving at Dynamo as a young boy, I'd been afraid of letting him down and that's what I felt I'd done. I hoped there would be no hard feelings between us. I owed the man my life and I knew that he'd risked everything to help me. How had I repaid him? By running away – that's how. I felt like a child again when I called at his apartment to say goodbye, struggling to put into words the gratitude I felt. In the end, I settled for just a few.

"Thank you," I said. "Thank you for everything."

With that, he smiled and shook my hand. I never saw him again. Two months later, he was found dead, having crashed his car into a tree on a straight stretch of road. Apparently, his blood alcohol levels were over three times the legal limit. When I heard the awful news, I felt not just an overwhelming sense of sorrow but a cold bolt of fear too. All the times I'd thought that I was being followed by the Stasi, had I been being paranoid after all? It had never been proved but I didn't believe that Muller's death was an accident. Not for a minute. I turn the pages of my file and find what I'm looking for.

Surveillance of defectors Karl Littman and Anders Muller

Informant (f) reports that he has Littman and Muller under close supervision in West Germany. The informant is of the firm belief that neither subject has any regrets about their ill-considered move and are extremely unlikely to return to the GDR. With regards to Littman, informants (U) and (I) consider all potential opportunities to use his parents to persuade him to return have now been exhausted although mail will still be intercepted.

Informant (f) will now put into motion plans to fulfil the wishes of our superior, Erich Meier and bring about the elimination of Karl Littman. To avoid suspicion, the elimination of Anders Muller should be delayed for the foreseeable future. Further information will follow with regards to this matter. At the earliest opportunity, it is recommended that an agent of the state should abduct Littman and force him to consume large amounts of alcohol spiked with poison that acts on the nerve cells. The agent should then allow Littman to make his escape only for him to be 'flashed' by a secondary agent, forcing him to lose control of the vehicle. It is of the utmost importance that Karl Littman's death is thought of as a tragic accident.

The twenty-five years that have passed since Muller's death can't numb the pain and guilt I feel. It should have been me in that car. I was the one that Meier wanted dead and once I was out of the picture, he settled for Muller instead. My eyes stinging with the tears that have now filled them, I slump back in my chair and take a minute to remember the man who helped me start my second life. I will leave Berlin tomorrow and I'm not sure if I will ever return. Like I said, there are just too many ghosts here. Some who I loved and others like Erich Meier who I despised. After German reunification, Meier was prosecuted and convicted for murders he had committed as far back as the 1930's. He eventually died behind bars two years ago.

As far as my family are concerned, after I moved to America, we had no contact for almost twenty years. Then, completely out of the blue, my father wrote to me. How he managed to find me, I didn't know. Too much time has already been lost he told me. It was important that we allowed old wounds to heal. He didn't expect me to return to visit the family in Berlin but he would very much like it, if he could bring my mother and Heidi over to America to see me. I wrote back that very night. I explained that I wanted to repair the damage that had been done all those years ago. It was important that we all looked forward rather than back into the past and I wanted my own son to know his grandparents and his auntie.

Within my letter, I enclosed five tickets for a flight to New York and three weeks later I met them at the airport. It hasn't been easy to get to know them again but we've all agreed we're going to work on it and we won't lose each other again.

As I shut my Stasi file, I feel I can finally close that chapter of my life. I have so much to look forward to now. Life in America is good and I'm enjoying watching my boy grow up. Despite my reservations, he's football mad himself and when I watched him score his first goal the other day, I felt my heart leap. After all these years, my love for football is beginning to return.

The Wartime Winger

*"Imagine it Jim - champions of the world.
That'd be alrightwouldn't it?"*

Growing up in the North of England in the 1930's, Jimmy Evans and his best friend Stan share a burning ambition to play for England in the World Cup. After years of hard work, and against the odds, it seems like their dream may even come true as they are tipped for a call up to the national team. However, a terrible new war is brewing. When Jimmy and Stan are finally asked to represent their country, it will be in the skies of Europe and not on the football pitch."

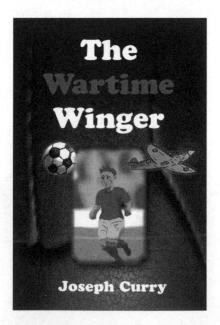

ISBN: 9781906132156   **£7.99**